Gina Charles lives in New Jersey with her husband, Francois. They have two grown children, Lachlan and Sloan, and have enjoyed living in and exploring multiple states. As an empty nester, she decided to write that book as she had always dreamed of writing. Gina has a BA in English and Communication and MA in English/Writing from the University of Dayton. She spent her first few professional years working as a television news producer before switching professions and working as a print editor. She spent the next 20 years "working" as a mother and volunteering for multiple organizations.

For my wonderful husband, Francois, and my incredible children, Lachlan and Sloan.

Gina Charles

LIFE'S LOVE SONG

AUSTIN MACAULEY PUBLISHERS™

LONDON • CAMBRIDGE • NEW YORK • SHARJAH

Ordering Information
Quantity sales: Special discounts are available on quantity purchases by corporations, associations, and others. For details, contact the publisher at the address below.

Publisher's Cataloging-in-Publication data
Charles, Gina
Life's Love Song

ISBN 9798891551541 (Paperback)
ISBN 9798891551558 (Hardback)
ISBN 9798891551565 (ePub e-book)

Library of Congress Control Number: 2023921563

www.austinmacauley.com/us

First Published 2024
Austin Macauley Publishers LLC
40 Wall Street, 33rd Floor, Suite 3302
New York, NY 10005
USA

mail-usa@austinmacauley.com
+1 (646) 5125767

<h1 style="text-align:center">1</h1>

Duncan was in the basement rec room playing video games, at that moment enjoying the latest version of his favorite football game. When he played video games, he was unaware of anything around him. It wasn't that he was intentionally being rude; he just wasn't capable of hearing what was going on around him. He didn't hear the radio playing his favorite song. And he certainly didn't hear his mother calling him from upstairs. Not until she came and yanked the cord from the TV was he even aware of her presence in the house.

"Hey! What are you doing? I was winning 61 to 7! That's my best ever!"

"I'm sorry, Duncan. That was the only way I could get your attention. You weren't listening to me," his mother Sheila sternly explained.

"I didn't hear you!" he whined a little too loudly.

"Well, then, that's a problem. Have you finished your homework?"

"No—Twenty more minutes," Duncan begged.

"Now. Twenty minutes always turns into 60. Then I'm back down here making the same threats. It's early in the year, but unless you want to do 7th grade again, you need to start taking your schoolwork more seriously. Let's get off on the right foot."

"Hmph!"

It wasn't that Duncan was a bad kid. In many ways, he was a typical 12-year-old boy, more interested in playing in the moment than worrying about the future. He wanted to do what he wanted when he wanted, without considering possible repercussions.

In fact, despite the pushback he often gave his mom, Duncan really was a good kid. He was very caring to his friends and to other people. He even loved his sister, though he rarely acted like it. With his outgoing personality, good looks—even at age 12—and athletic talent, he was very popular at school and with other peers. His shoulder-length black wavy hair was always a mess, but his strong cheekbones and brilliant blue eyes drew attention from the tangled web on his head.

He was smart when he wanted to be and skated through school by putting forth half an effort much of the time. His teachers and his parents always told him if he would try as hard in school as he did on the playground, he'd do very well in school. Duncan just hadn't found that to be very important yet.

As Duncan climbed the stairs to head for his room, he kicked the steps and grumbled to himself, still furious at his mother. Sheila sighed and shook her head. She'd been through this routine many times over the past few years, always questioning herself about what she'd done wrong.

Sheila knew she'd spoiled Duncan and his 14-year-old sister, Maddie. While she grew up in a family with an abundance of love, her family didn't have much money. Her parents were always worried about how they were going to pay their bills, and Sheila often went to bed hungry. It wasn't that her parents didn't feed her. Her mother always made a good dinner, which her parents, Sheila, and her two brothers ate together. However, with two older brothers, she didn't always get enough of that good dinner.

When Sheila fell in love with her now-husband Jake—and he actually loved her back—it was almost too good to be true. They met in college, Sheila working her way through with two jobs, financial aid, and several student loans. It was their senior year when Jake walked into the school cafeteria where Sheila worked. Jake usually ate off campus but was meeting a friend in the cafeteria to study. He found much more than he was looking for that day.

Jake looked at Sheila as she was clearing the table beside him. "Wow!" was all he could say.

"Excuse me?" she responded.

"I'm sorry," Jake muttered. "I'm Jake. You just took me by surprise. You have such beautiful blue eyes." He laughed at himself. "Boy, that sounds like a cheesy pickup line. I don't mean to sound that way, but you really are stunning."

Sheila loved everything about Jake instantly. He was a bit goofy, stumbling and falling over his words as he tried to charm her that day. Jake had had a much different childhood than Sheila. While Sheila's family struggled to pay bills and survive on anything but their love, Jake had grown up with money and everything he wanted. Yet, his parents had raised him to appreciate what he had and to respect everyone else as equal, regardless of financial status.

Jake's good looks were a cliché: tall, dark, and handsome, with black hair, a dark complexion, and eyes such dark brown that they often looked black. That could be why he was so taken with Sheila's eyes.

It wasn't that she was so beautiful in any other way. Really, she was quite average in build and facial structure. At least, that's how *she* saw herself. She knew she shouldn't be so critical of her looks, but as a 22-year-old, self-proclaimed book nerd, she still hadn't found that self-confidence to see her own external beauty, except for her eyes. Her hair was a drab light brown, but her eyes resembled the color of the ocean Jake often saw when his family visited the Caribbean.

After graduation, Sheila and Jake moved to Chicago, where Sheila worked as a copy editor for an environmental magazine and Jake worked for a Wall Street firm. After some careful planning for their future, Sheila and Jake were married two years later. Five years later, Maddie was born, and Sheila stopped working. She wanted to stay home with her kids.

Sheila was totally dedicated to doing the best she could for Maddie and Jake, and she couldn't imagine a better life. Thanks to their careful financial planning, with Maddie's birth, came a home in Highland Park. Sheila had what she could only imagine and dream of as a child. Every morning, Jake got up and went to a great job.

Meanwhile, Sheila spent her day with Maddie; they went everywhere together. Because Sheila was in a new neighborhood, she was anxious to meet friends, so once Maddie turned 6 months old, Sheila enrolled her in her first gym class, where Mommy and Daughter met their first friends. Their best friends were Claire and her daughter, Gabby, who was just 3 months older than Maddie.

The four of them were together almost every day. Together, with some other friends from the Gym Tots class, they formed a playgroup, joined a music class, and later, when they were a little older, even joined an art class. Sheila really wanted Maddie to have everything she didn't have as a child.

Just a little more than 2 years later, Duncan was born. Sheila was ecstatic: She had a girl and a boy! From the get-go, Duncan was a charmer, with his dark curls and Sheila's blue eyes. And he was given the same wonderful childhood that Maddie was given.

At 2½, Maddie started a 3-hour preschool program 3 days a week, and Sheila was able to spend the same quality time with Duncan that she did with Maddie. The three of them then spent their afternoons at the park or with friends. The children were never in need or want of anything. They had everything they wanted—and so did Sheila.

2

Once Sheila had finally gotten Duncan upstairs to do his homework, her next chore was to get Maddie home. As a freshman, Maddie had moved up from middle school to high school, where she was excited to meet the older kids, especially the boys. Luckily, her best friend Gabby had been along for the ride, attending the same schools as Maddie since they first started back in preschool. Maddie had gone home with Gabby after school that day to talk about their new adventures and, of course, the cute boys they'd seen.

Maddie and Gabby had been almost inseparable since they first met in that mommy-and-me gym class. It had been an immediate bond, and after all of these years of friendship, they even resembled each other in looks with the same long, dark brown hair. Maddie's hair required a little more maintenance with a morning blowout to tame the frizzier, thicker hair. Gabby could let her hair dry naturally, much to Maddie's chagrin. "No fair," she complained to her best friend.

People often confused the two of them when first meeting them, but upon closer inspection, they didn't look alike. For one thing, Maddie had her father's almost-black eyes, while Gabby's were hazel. "And I'm taller," Maddie would tease Gabby. After all, Maddie was 5 feet 3-¾ inches, while Gabby was only 5 feet 3-½ inches. This reminder always prompted an eye roll from Gabby.

Sheila picked up the phone and called.

"Hello?" answered the voice on the other end of the phone.

"Hi, Claire. Is my daughter about ready to come home?"

"Ha! Are those two ever ready to be separated? But I guess it's about that time. I actually have to run to the store, so I'll drop her off on my way."

"Are you sure, Claire?" Even after 14 years of friendship, Sheila still hated to impose on Claire.

"Stop it! Yes, I'm sure," Claire answered.

"OK, thanks. See you in a few minutes."

Sheila spent the next few minutes chopping vegetables and reflecting on her friendship with Claire, thankful she had someone with whom to share the joys and tribulations of motherhood.

Gabby and Maddie were in Gabby's room with the doors locked. They spent hours alone in that room, and their parents never understood what they did for so long together in one room. "We just talk," they always explained.

Then again, teenage girls do have much to talk about. Boys, being the number-one subject, was again their subject of conversation today. One boy in particular—a junior named Eli—had caught Maddie's attention that day.

Maddie was walking out of her pre-calculus class when she saw Eli leaving the room across the hall. She knew who Eli was because he was a varsity football and basketball player. However, as a freshman, she had never met him, or even seen him in such close proximity.

To Maddie's surprise, Eli smiled and said hello to her. She was so shocked that she had to check the doorway behind her to make sure Eli was actually talking to her. She smiled and squeaked a quiet hello back. This short encounter, of course, prompted hours of speculation and conversation between Maddie and her faithful confidant Gabby.

A quick knock on the door brought the girls back to reality. Maddie, in fact, wasn't the girlfriend of a star athlete at school—at least not yet. She was, instead, Maddie Trestin, who needed to get home to do her homework.

When Maddie got home, she ran right up to her room. Between doodling 'Mrs. Elijah Schwartz' or just 'Maddie Schwartz', she managed to get a little homework done before dinner.

Jake walked in from work as Sheila was coaxing Maddie out of her room to come downstairs for dinner. One thing Sheila had no problem doing was getting Duncan to stop his homework for dinner. He was already downstairs, waiting for the rest of them. Maddie was an entirely different story. She loved her family more than anything but was at that age when she really valued her independence and quiet time alone in her room.

However, she looked up with a smile when Jake slowly opened her door. She was still a "daddy's little girl" at heart.

3

"Hurry up! I'm starving," Duncan yelled from the kitchen. He had discovered by now that his mother had made tacos, a family favorite, for dinner. It was unusual for Duncan to be surprised by a dinner menu because, as a 12-year-old boy, "What's for dinner?" was pretty much an everyday question. "Finally," he grumbled as the rest of the family staggered in to make their plates.

Talking about their days was a required discussion at the Trestin family dinner table. The conversation that evening dragged on with descriptions of pretty uneventful days at home, school, and work: the first high school test for which Maddie had studied all weekend, a basketball game in PE that highlighted Duncan's school day, a couple hours in the school library where Sheila was able to chat with the librarian, and a long conference call with the New York office that dragged on for most of Jake's day.

"Hmmm," Jake thought aloud. "It seems like this family could use a little excitement. It's still pretty warm for this late in September. Why don't we have a pool party this weekend? It will be a nice distraction from all the humdrum of life."

"Cool! Can we invite whoever we want?" Duncan cut off his father.

Sheila grumbled 'whomever' under her breath but quickly added, "Sure. Why not!"

Of course, Maddie's first thought was about how she could get Eli to their party but quickly realized that she hadn't even mumbled more than a hello to him in the hallway. And she almost couldn't even squeak that out. How on earth could she possibly be thinking of a way to get him to their party? "That's ridiculous," escaped her lips before she realized what she was doing.

"What? Why not, Maddie? Do you have something else going on this weekend? What's so ridiculous about inviting over some friends this weekend? It will be a nice way to say goodbye to the summer," her confused father inquired.

"Oh! I'm sorry. I was just thinking of something else to myself. I think it's a great idea. May I help you plan the menu, Mom? And I'd love to make some cookies."

"Alright. Sheila, you and Maddie can take care of ordering or cooking the food, I'll call Troy to see whether he can lifeguard, and Duncan, you set up the volleyball and badminton nets."

It was pretty much the standard protocol for parties at the Trestin household. No further instruction was needed. Everyone knew where to jump in and how to do their parts.

"Obviously, you can take care of your own invitations yourselves. I'm sure you kids are both anxious to start texting as soon as dinner is over. Please try to stick to a reasonable number of people. We don't need 500 people here on Saturday," Jake warned.

"Don't even say that number, Jake, or they'll think 400 is quite acceptable," Shelia joked. "But seriously, please give me a head count as soon as you can so that I know how much food to have."

Maddie and Duncan quickly jumped up and started to run to their rooms to find their phones. (*No phones at the dinner table* was a strict rule.)

"Get back here! Clear the table and load the dishwasher before you go. It's the least you could do for your mother," Jake ordered his excited children.

Maddie and Duncan were soon in their rooms after a haphazard rinsing and loading of the dishes. Duncan's list was very quickly and easily assembled—at 12, he had no interest in girls. He narrowed it down to his 15 best friends. Including Duncan, 16 boys were plenty to spread out across the volleyball and badminton courts and still have a few left to shoot hoops in the driveway.

Now that the kids were older, pool games were prohibited. "The stupid girls won't let us jump around. They're too worried we might splash them," Duncan had to explain to his entourage every time they had a party. "It is a pool, after all! It's meant for getting wet!"

While Duncan speedily sent a group text to his friends, Maddie FaceTimed Gabby. Her guest list wasn't going to be as easy, and she needed Gabby's input. At 14, she *was* interested in the opposite sex and needed to mull over who exactly was the right mix of boys and girls.

"I know! Let's invite Eli," were the first words out of Gabby's mouth.

"Gabby, don't be silly. What would I say to him, 'I know you don't know me but want to come over and hang out with a bunch of 7th and 9th graders? Oh! And a bunch of old people?'"

"Don't roll your eyes at me, Maddie! How better to get his attention than to show him how fun you and your family are?"

"No," Maddie snapped back sharply.

With that discussion quickly over, the girls spent the next 90 minutes making a list. Some of the invitees were obvious and didn't require contemplation. Others had to be debated, added to the list, debated some more, and subtracted from the list. After all, the girls had to consider who liked whom and who had broken hearts caused by whom. It was a tangled web to be untangled.

The week seemed to drag by for Maddie and Duncan. They were so excited for what would probably be the last big hurrah of the summer. The week flew by for Sheila, who had to make most of the arrangements for the day. She enjoyed making most of the food by herself and relied very little on catered foods that had been prepared in advance. Luckily, Maddie would help her with some of the cooking and baking. Duncan: She would have to keep from eating all the food as she prepared it.

Sure enough, the day did finally arrive, and it was a beauty! The entire month of September had been unseasonably warm, and Saturday, September 26, was no different. Despite its being less than a week until October, the temperature was supposed to be in the mid-80s.

"That's perfect," Duncan exclaimed as soon as he heard the weather forecast. "I want everyone drenched in sweat before jumping into the pool."

"That's disgusting," Maddie spat at him.

"Oh, shut up. You and Gabby will be drooling over those sweaty boys that you invited. You know they are going to ditch you to come play with me and my friends for most of the party."

"*You* shut up, Duncan! Why would they want to go play with little boys?"

Sheila was not in the mood: "You two, stop. Either go where I can't hear you, or better yet, stop bickering! Actually, even better yet, Duncan, go help your dad set up the tables in the yard. Maddie, you help me get the plates and utensils set out. Then you can put all of your cookies on a platter."

The Trestin family loved having pool parties and barbeques for their friends and family, so they were pretty much a well-oiled machine when it came to prepping for them. Their parents just occasionally had to steer Maddie and Duncan away from the little sibling spats and toward their party chores.

By 11 a.m., everything was set and ready, and the guests started to arrive. The kids and their groups segregated themselves accordingly. Duncan was wrong. Maddie's male friends didn't have much interest in playing with the younger boys that day. Not when cute girls in swimsuits were their other option.

The weather was perfect, the food was perfect, the guest lists were perfect, and everyone was having a great time. The day was flying by, and everyone wanted it to last as long as it possibly could. They knew their days of summer were limited, so no one was leaving that day until it was time to drag themselves home to bed.

It was about 4:00 when everyone was starting to think about hitting the food tables for an afternoon snack when two uninvited guests (or at least uninvited by anyone in the Trestin family) walked through the side gate and around the house to the backyard.

Maddie was deep in conversation with a group of girls, discussing the very important topic of the dating reality show they all couldn't get enough of, when she saw Gabby's mouth drop open. Maddie quickly turned around to see Eli Schwartz and his best friend Michael Silkora standing on the outskirts of the party looking around.

"What have you done, Gabby?" Maddie shot a quick accusatory look at her best friend.

"Well, what's done is done. Don't just stand there, Maddie. You have to go over there."

"What on earth do I say? I didn't even invite them here. I can't believe they showed up." Maddie froze for a moment. "I'm too scared. I can't go."

"Come on. Olivia, Sophia, and I will go with you. We can all stumble through it together. Let's go, girls." Gabby grabbed her best friend's hand and gave her a little tug.

Maddie looked over again and saw her dad starting to walk toward Eli and Michael.

"Oh, no!" she yelped. "OK. Let's go!" She was desperate to reach the boys before her father did.

The four girls made a quick beeline to the two older boys who had wandered over to the cooler by the drink table to grab a bottle of water.

"Uh, hi," Maddie squeaked out. *"Darn it. Quit talking like a little mouse,"* she complained internally. Then cheerfully, she added, "What are you guys doing here? How did you know we were having a party?"

Michael answered first: "Gabby told us about it."

"I hope you don't mind that we stopped by," Eli finally said something.

"Of course not. It's great. I just hope you don't mind that none of your friends is here. It's just my friends and a bunch of my annoying brother's pesky friends."

"I don't mind at all, Maddie." Eli looked around. "I see some guys here that are on the football team with me." He paused and looked around again, then looked straight into Maddie's eyes. "But I mostly just came to see you, anyway."

Maddie felt her face turn 18 shades of red. She couldn't believe what she was hearing and hoped this wasn't some type of cruel joke. She stood dumbfounded and didn't realize she was still staring right into Eli's eyes.

After several awkward seconds, Gabby secretly kicked her friend to startle her out of her daze and decided she better jump in to help. "Are you guys hungry? Maddie and her mom made a ton of food. Maddie is a really good cook! Or do you want to cool off? The water is perfect."

"These cookies look really good. I think I'll just have one of them for now." Eli grabbed a cookie and took a huge bite. "Delicious."

Maddie, still in a state of shock, couldn't believe what was happening, but just in case it was real, she decided she better come to life. "Thanks, Eli. I made those cookies. They are my specialty. I took an old recipe and made some alterations to them to make them my own."

About then, Duncan looked over and noticed the latecomers. He was also dumbfounded, wondering why on earth the captain of the football team was at his party. While Duncan was still in middle school, he certainly knew who Eli was. He planned on following in his shoes someday. The middle school didn't have a football team, but he had already played several seasons of flag football.

Duncan trotted over to see what was going on. "Hi. I'm Duncan. Why are *you* here?"

"Duncan! That's a rude question!" Maddie quickly scolded her brother.

"That's OK. Hi, Duncan. I'm Eli, and this is Michael. We came to see your sister and her friends."

"Why? What would you want to do with them?"

"Well, why not? I like your sister so far. She seems pretty cool."

"OK," Duncan conceded. "If you want to shoot hoops or something later, we have a lot of games going on."

"We just might do that. Thanks."

Duncan ran off to play some more volleyball. Much to his friends' chagrin, he had put the game on hold to run over to check out the situation. His friends had to do what Duncan wanted. "My house. My rules," he loved to remind them.

Despite Maddie's usual desire to not want Duncan anywhere near her and her friends, she was actually grateful for his little interruption. It had given her another minute to collect herself.

"Do you want to come say hi to some of the guys?" She led Eli and Michael over to another group of her friends. Some of them were on the football team, so she knew they would know Eli and Michael. They could all talk about football, which would be a great icebreaker. Gabby, Olivia, and Sophia joined them, and before they knew it, they were all engaged in conversation and laughing.

Maddie still had to pinch herself occasionally to convince herself this was all happening. *Freshman year might be alright after all. It might even be more than alright,* she thought to herself.

Across the yard, Duncan was also having the time of his life. He was in his element—a yard full of friends playing sports. Could life be any better?

4

Jake walked in the door that Monday afternoon at 4:30. He startled Sheila. He was home at least three hours earlier than he usually got home, and he hadn't even called her to say he was coming home early.

"What are you doing here, Jake? Is everything OK? You just about gave me a heart attack."

"Um—no, Sheila, actually everything is not OK, but I'm sure it will be again soon enough."

"Jake, you are scaring me."

"I'm sorry. I don't want to scare you, but be prepared for what I'm about to tell you," Jake sighed, paused, and took a deep breath. "I just lost my job."

"What?" Sheila gasped. "Why? How did this happen? You didn't have any idea, did you? What are you going to do?"

"Slow down, Sheila. No, I had no idea. No warning! What a great way to treat an employee who has been with the company for 10 years. Remember that all-day call with the New York office that I mentioned last week? It was basically a check-in with all the departments to find out the status of projects taking place, who's doing what, and so on. The company is going through a major restructuring, combining Chicago and New York departments and consolidating work that's spread out corporatewide. Several people from our office are being relocated to New York. Those of us with higher salaries are being let go."

"Oh, no! What are we going to do, Jake?" Sheila's eyes were starting to tear up a little. Not only was she worried about not having an income, but she also felt very bad about what had happened to her husband. Jake was a very hard worker and had given every second he could to that job. It was so unfair.

"Don't worry," Jake tried to comfort her. "I'm very angry, but I'm not too worried about finding another job. I'm very good at what I do. I'm sure someone will want me. It's just going to be a hassle trying to find that perfect job again. And for that perfect salary. In the meantime, they gave me a pretty nice severance package. I'll be getting a big check at the end of the week. And our health insurance will continue for a while. They are letting me go immediately so that I can start looking for something else."

"Jake, the kids are going to be home any minute now. What are you going to tell them?"

"I've actually been thinking that I shouldn't tell them anything just yet. The school year is not even a month in, Maddie is settling into the high school, and Duncan needs to have as little distraction as possible. Let's just keep it a secret for a bit. Maybe I can find something else before we even have to tell them."

"Are you sure that's the best idea? We're usually so upfront and honest with them," Sheila questioned.

Just then, the front door burst open, and Duncan tore full force through the living room and down the hall to the kitchen. The refrigerator was always his first stop after getting home from school. Maddie walked in right after him.

"Dad, what are you doing here? Isn't it a little early for you to be gracing our presence?" Maddie asked.

"Oh! Hi, Dad. I didn't even see you there," Duncan added.

"Hi. Uhhh—I actually had a meeting offsite today, and it ended a little early. Instead of fighting the traffic to get back downtown, I decided to just take the rest of the day off," Jake fumbled through an explanation.

"That's very rare and unusual for you, Dad. Are you feeling OK?" Maddie joked, although she was a little suspicious.

"Yes, I'm fine, but since I'm home early, why don't you both get busy with your homework and get done as soon as you can. Do a good job, of course, but if you can get done at a reasonable hour, maybe we can all cuddle up later and watch a movie together. We might as well make use of my short day to do something fun."

"I get to pick the movie!" Duncan yelled, as he grabbed the turkey sandwich he had already thrown together and ran off to his room. He usually liked to kill a little time and decompress after school by playing video games and pushing his homework back until after dinner, but he loved watching movies with his dad. He sat down at his desk and started his math homework, trying not to get mustard on his paper.

With the kids both upstairs in their rooms, Sheila and Jake quietly continued their conversation. Sheila pulled out a chicken from the fridge as Jake sat at the kitchen table with his laptop.

"Where are you going to look? Do you have any idea who might be hiring?" Sheila asked quietly.

"I'm going to do a little research right now at the table. And I guess I'll actually do that as long as I need. I'll also make a list of people to call. If I do some networking, someone will certainly know about something. I have a lot of contacts."

Sheila went through the motions of making dinner, but her mind was elsewhere. Jake seemed very confident that he'd have no problem finding another job, and Sheila had confidence in him.

However, Jake had been very successful in his job. She knew there couldn't be that many positions open for him. Once you get so close to the top of the managerial pyramid, fewer and fewer spots become available. She also hated the thought that the family might have to relocate to another city for him to find a new position. They were so happy in their life where it was.

Sheila's mind couldn't find anything else to think about. All she could do was worry for the next couple of hours as she mindlessly threw together dinner. She loved to cook and loved making dinner for her family, but this evening she needed something easy. She was so preoccupied with worry that she feared she'd cut off a finger if she really tried to make too much. A simple roasted chicken, rice pilaf, and honey-glazed carrots would have to do. Her family loved Sheila's cooking, and what seemed like an easy dinner to Sheila seemed like a gourmet meal to the rest of them.

After they had eaten and the kids had loaded the dishwasher, they ran to the family room.

"I'm actually giving you a choice," Duncan exclaimed. The other Trestins couldn't believe their ears. Duncan had called movie rights, and he wasn't usually so quick to relinquish those rights without an argument. "Anything Christopher Nolan!"

They all laughed. Christopher Nolan was the family's favorite director and moviemaker, and they'd seen all of his movies too many times to count. They were all happy with that choice and quickly decided on *Inception*.

5

Duncan had no problem quickly losing himself in the movie he had seen countless times, and even Jake was able to escape his worries for the next few hours. Sheila, however, still couldn't shake her worry and was completely lost in her thoughts for the first hour of the movie, until the sound of Maddie's phone jerked her back to awareness.

Maddie grabbed her phone quickly. "Oh! May I please go answer this in my room? I've seen the movie so many times anyway, and it's not like we're actually spending quality time talking or anything?"

"Go ahead, Maddie," her father gave her permission.

Maddie ran up the stairs two at a time quickly to get out of hearing distance.

"Hello?" She tried not to sound too out of breath or too excited. She knew it was Eli calling because they had exchanged numbers at the party.

"Are you OK? You sound all out of breath. Are you out for a run or something?" Eli teased her.

Maddie giggled: "No. I just ran upstairs to get to my room. My family and I were watching a movie."

"That's a nice luxury for a Monday night."

"I know, right? My dad got home from work really early today. It was weird. He never gets home as early as he did tonight. He told Duncan and me to get our homework done, and we'd have an early movie night."

"I'm sorry," Eli apologized. "Do you want me to let you go? I don't want to make you miss the movie."

"No. No," Maddie tried to sound nonchalant. "I've seen the movie a million times before."

Maddie quickly relaxed and fell into an easy conversation with Eli. She realized she didn't really know much about him, other than he was a popular and handsome kid at school—the most handsome, in her opinion. What she didn't realize was that she was rapidly firing questions at him.

"Slow down," he told her and laughed. "I want to know more about you, too. I don't just want to talk about myself the entire night."

As they exchanged life stories, Maddie was still much more interested in what he had to say than sharing what she thought were boring facts about her own life. She learned that Eli had been born in California and had moved to Chicago when he was in the 6th grade.

He left a large and diverse family in California for his mother to take a job as a law professor at the University of Chicago. She had worked at a large firm in Los Angeles but decided she wanted more time with her family and thought teaching would give her that option. Eli's father was in sales and didn't have any trouble making the move and finding a good job in Chicago.

Maddie thought her ancestry was boring so loved hearing that his parents were both mixed race—his mom was African American and Japanese, and his dad was African American and Caucasian.

"My grandfather was Jewish, but my father didn't really continue with any type of religion once my grandparents were divorced when he was very young. But I love being such a mish-mosh of so many different races and religions," he explained. "My mom is Christian, and so am I. She used to take me to church in LA, but we never really found a church in Chicago. I think my background is why I like people so much—from all different places, different cultures, different religions."

"I think you are the best of everything," Maddie blushed as she explained, "I mean, you look good—really good— and are very distinctive looking. And it really comes out in your personality that you like everyone and are super accepting of everyone. That's cool."

Maddie was very disappointed when Eli told her, "Well, I better go, Maddie. You might have gotten your homework done, but I haven't even started mine yet. I got home from practice and ate, then decided I needed a little more downtime, so I called you. I have an APUSH exam tomorrow, and I have a bunch more studying to do."

"A what 'push'?"

"Oh!" Eli laughed. "I keep forgetting you are a freshman. You just don't seem like one. You don't know all the class terminology yet. Don't worry. You'll learn it soon enough. APUSH is short for, in its longest definition, Advanced Placement United States History."

"Well, that sounds fun," Maddie said sarcastically. "I'll let you go study. Maybe I'll see you tomorrow at school."

"I hope so," was the answer she hoped for and was the answer she heard from the other end of the line. That answer also sent her into a daydream for the next several minutes. Could Eli possibly like her?

He seemed so nice and didn't seem like the kind of guy who would mess with her just for the fun of it. Maddie saw herself cheering for Eli at the next football game, sitting in the stands as his girlfriend during basketball season, and even going to Prom—as a freshman! She had to snap herself out of it and tell herself not to get too far ahead of herself or she might end up brokenhearted.

Instead of running back downstairs to the movie and her family, Maddie decided she better talk to Gabby about what had happened. She tried to FaceTime Gabby, but she didn't answer, so Maddie went back downstairs to finish watching the movie. But her mind wasn't with Cobb, Arthur, and Ariadne on the screen; it was back at Prom, which was still many months away.

6

Sheila tossed and turned most of the night and couldn't believe when Jake started snoring about 30 seconds after climbing into bed. *I guess that's just the difference between us,* she thought. *He sleeps to escape his worries, while I lie here awake worrying enough for both of us.*

She felt as though she had just finally fallen asleep when Jake jumped out of bed at 6:00.

"What are you doing? It's not like you have to rush to the office this morning," Sheila inquired.

"I know, honey, but I really don't want the kids to know what's going on. I don't want them to know I lost my job until maybe after I find another one. They aren't used to seeing me in the morning, so I'm going to head out early and try to do a little networking. I was already able to set up a couple of meetings today. I have one at 9:00, so I'll head out and kill a little time before then. I'll come back home for a while once I know it's safe and the kids are gone."

"That's good. I'm glad to see you in such good spirits. I barely slept a wink last night," Sheila yawned as she spoke. "Are you meeting with anyone I know?"

"Not really. At 9:00, I'm meeting with an analyst I know at another firm. His name is Ted, but you wouldn't have any way of knowing him. Then I actually have a meeting with a headhunter at 3:00."

"How were you able to set up these meetings so quickly? Last I knew, you didn't have anything planned."

"I know," Jake replied enthusiastically. "It all happened in the short time while you were making dinner last night. Then we were with the kids for dinner, then the movie. I was just so exhausted last night that I fell asleep before I could even tell you."

"Well, maybe I would have slept a little better if you had shared some good, or at least promising, news with me. I'm exhausted."

"Why don't you take a little nap after the kids leave?"

"I can't," Sheila sighed and rolled her eyes. "A mammogram this morning. My favorite thing to do."

"Yikes," Jake sympathized. "Tell me no more. I'll see you at home then after both of our 'meetings'." He made air quotes to downplay Sheila's appointment as just a meeting.

Jake quickly showered and escaped the house before Maddie and Duncan got up and knew any better. Sheila, still dragging, helped the kids with breakfast and then drove them to school. It was her turn in the carpool, so she also picked up the twin boys a couple of blocks over. Normally, she would head to the gym for her spin class after drop-off, but she went home to shower and get ready for her appointment.

The rest of her morning and appointment were pretty uneventful. She was actually excited, despite the circumstances, to get a little alone time with her husband that afternoon. She stopped at their favorite sandwich shop and picked up some lunch for them. "Why not have a little 'date' and forget about everything for a bit?" she asked herself.

When she walked into the house, Jake was already there and was watching the baseball highlights from the night before. He hadn't watched his beloved Cubs' game the night before because he was watching the movie. "Argh. It's not looking so good for the playoffs this year."

Jake was happy to see Sheila, but he seemed a little down, considering how optimistic he had been that morning.

"You OK?" Sheila asked. "There's always next year. As a Cubs fan, you get used to telling yourself that."

Jake gave a quick laugh. He didn't want to sound too discouraged but also wanted to be honest with his wife. "It's not the Cubs. I thought I'd hear a little better news from Ted this morning. I guess it's just a bad time to be without a job. It seems like a lot of firms are consolidating offices, and I'm not the only one out there looking for a job."

Sheila's heart sank, but she didn't want Jake to know it. "It's OK, honey. It's just your first meeting. We hoped it would happen quickly and easily, but that was probably unrealistic. You still have your meeting this afternoon. Maybe that will go better. In the meantime, I stopped and got your favorite tuna salad sandwich. Let's eat. I'm starving."

"Me, too. Thank you, sweetheart. You know me so well." Jake stood up and kissed his wife on the cheek and accompanied her to the kitchen table.

Jake and Sheila sat and enjoyed their alone time. They took so little of it for themselves. Any free time they usually spent with the kids. It was nice just to sit and talk for a while.

They focused on the kids and steered all conversation away from the job search.

"What do you know about those two older boys who showed up at the party on Saturday?" Jake inquired. "Maddie and Gabby seemed pretty interested in them."

"I'm not surprised. They are pretty cute," Sheila laughed. "I don't know much about them. I know they are juniors, so I was pretty surprised to see them walk in. We'll have to find out more from Duncan. Maddie will probably resist if we ask her."

"I'm sure she will," Jake agreed. "Duncan, on the other hand, will be all too happy to share any details he knows about them, especially if he thinks we are trying to pry into Maddie's business."

7

Maddie and Gabby practically ran out the front doors of the school. They had different lunch periods that day, so they still hadn't had a chance to catch up after Maddie's phone date with Eli the night before. They'd only had the chance to quickly plan a trip to Antonia's, the local coffee shop, immediately after school.

"I still can't believe you didn't answer my FaceTime last night, Gabby," Maddie pretended to be angry.

"I know! I was so bummed when I saw I missed it, but it was too late to call back once my mom gave my phone back. She was worried about my *Beowulf* reading, so she took my phone away. What good did that do? I still barely understood any of it, even after *trying* to give it my full attention!"

"Ugh," Maddie agreed. "Why do we need to read that ancient garbage?"

"Well, enough about *Beowulf.* I can't wait to hear all the Eli details now," Gabby squealed.

Maddie pulled open the door of Antonia's and stopped abruptly. She had very quickly scanned the coffee shop to see whether anyone 'good' was already sitting down, and that's when she saw her father. He was facing the back wall

37

with a 20-something, very attractive woman. She couldn't see his face, but she could tell it was her father.

"What is he doing in this part of town? He isn't even wearing his suit! He's looking all handsome in his jeans and sweater. Who is this woman? Why isn't Mom with them? Oh, my gosh! Dad is having an affair!" So many thoughts rushed into her head as she made an about-face and practically pushed Gabby back out onto the sidewalk.

"Maddie! What's going on? You practically pushed me down," Gabby drilled her.

She quickly changed her tone when she saw all color had drained from Maddie's face, and she looked as though she were going to be sick.

"Maddie? Are you OK? Do you need to sit down?"

"No! We need to get away from here as quickly as possible."

Gabby couldn't believe it as Maddie described what she had seen: Jake sitting at a table in the middle of the afternoon when he should be downtown at work with a pretty woman laughing at him from the other side of the table. Gabby had known Maddie's father her entire life. Their families were as close as two families who weren't related could be.

"Come on, Maddie. There's no way. Your father wouldn't do that."

"I know that was my father, Gabby. It's not like I can't recognize him. That was him, and that was the sweater my grandparents gave him for Christmas. How could he?"

"There has to be a good explanation. Your father would never cheat on your mother, Maddie."

"Well, that's what I thought, too. But Mom did seem a little odd last night. I wonder if she knows! Or maybe she knows something is not right with my dad, but she doesn't know what. What should I do?"

"OK. Let's think and come up with a plan. I don't think you should tell your mom. Let's try to investigate first. How can we check up on your dad without his knowing it?"

"Oh, Gabby!" Maddie started to cry before she even knew the tears were about to erupt. "I thought my life was going so well. I had such a great talk with Eli last night." She paused to choke back sobs. "Now I'm not even in the mood to tell you about it. I just want to go home and see my mom. And I never want to see my dad again!"

Maddie and Gabby had made their way to a bench in the park across the street. They just sat there for an hour. Maddie sobbed, then stopped. Then she talked with Gabby a little, questioning why her father had come home early from work the night before and wondering whether he had come home from being with 'that woman' yesterday, too.

Finally, the girls decided they better get home. Their mothers had given them permission to get coffee together after school, but they'd be expecting them home by now. They decided to walk to the Trestin's house, so Gabby called her mom and asked to be picked up there in 30 minutes.

The girls talked very little on the walk. Maddie just didn't feel like talking about Eli and his call the night before. Her father had totally messed up her good mood and maybe even messed up her life!

Once Gabby had gotten into the car with Claire, Maddie wiped her eyes and gave herself a minute, hoping she could look normal and remain composed when she went inside and saw Sheila.

She failed.

"Maddie, what's wrong?" Sheila could tell immediately that Maddie had been crying. Mothers have a way of knowing, which actually isn't too hard when their daughters' eyes are red and smeared with the very little mascara they wear to school.

"Nothing, Mom. I just had a bad day at school. I really don't want to talk about it. I just want to go lie down for a little bit."

"OK, sweetheart. I'm here for you if you want to talk."

Sheila knew not to push it. When Maddie wanted to talk, she'd text her mom and ask her to come to her room. That's always how Maddie reached out and how Sheila knew when Maddie needed to get something off her chest.

Sheila grumbled to herself. "Just what I need. Something else to worry about!" She just couldn't shake the feeling that Maddie had had her heart broken. That's usually what happens when a freshman gets enamored with an upperclassman.

"Well, let me start thinking now of how I can talk to her about this," Sheila told herself. She had her heart broken many times in high school. It was a rite of passage that she expected her daughter would have to work through as well.

8

Duncan burst through the door soon after Maddie got home. Sheila was in the kitchen when she heard him calling.

Duncan had a meeting after school with other student athletes and the athletic department coaches. The fall season had barely begun, but the meeting was already to discuss winter sports. Fall sports practices had been delayed that day so that everyone could attend. The school wanted to make sure everyone understood what to expect over the coming months, and each coach spoke a bit about his or her winter sport.

Duncan didn't play a fall sport at school, since football didn't start until high school. Instead, he played flag football in a town rec league. As much as he loved flag football, he couldn't wait until freshman year for "real football". Until then, he was very excited just to play any sport for the school. Therefore, the meeting today was very exciting for him. He had stayed a little after the meeting to talk further with the middle school boys' basketball coach.

"Mom! My meeting was so awesome today! I met my coach. He played basketball at Ohio State!"

"Wow! That's great, Duncan. But slow down. Basketball hasn't started yet. You still have to make the team. And last time I checked, you were about to start your flag football season. One sport at a time, please."

Sheila always wanted to encourage Duncan, but she also wanted to make sure he didn't get ahead of himself. Duncan loved his sports, but his parents had to keep him grounded and make sure he was taking school seriously, as well.

As Duncan made a quick snack and sat down at the table, he continued to gush on about the basketball coach and how "cool" he was. Sheila was happy to have this conversation. It was a nice distraction from the bad news of the last couple of days. "At least one of my family members is in a good mental space," she assured herself.

Duncan gulped down the last swallow of milk, and Sheila sent him on his way, reminding him, "Hey—you got home late today, so no video games. Get right to your homework."

"But, Mom, I didn't get to play after school yesterday either. Can't I just have 30 minutes?"

"How about a compromise? You get 15 minutes. And don't forget, you didn't play yesterday because you were trying to knock out your homework early so that we could all watch the movie last night."

"Yeah, but—"

"15 minutes or nothing," Sheila cut him off.

"OK," Duncan moped as suddenly the door to the garage opened. "Dad, you're home early again?"

"Hi, buddy. Yep. I have a lot of offsite meetings right now, so I get to come home a little earlier."

"Cool! But I have to go get homework done." Duncan rolled his eyes. "Mom gave me a whopping 15 minutes to play games."

"Well, use it wisely."

"Then you can tell Dad all about your meeting over dinner tonight," Sheila chimed in, hoping to cut off Duncan before he started in about the meeting. She was anxious to talk to Jake in private.

Maddie heard her father come into the house downstairs. She had no interest in going down to see him. She decided to stay in her room until her mother called her down to dinner, even though she hadn't gotten her coffee and hadn't had anything to eat or drink since lunchtime at school. She had lost her appetite and wasn't hungry at all, but she sure could have used something to drink.

With Maddie and Duncan both in their rooms, Sheila had the chance to warn Jake about her exchange with Maddie.

"I'm sure it's probably something to do with that boy, Eli. Not necessarily, I guess. It could be someone or something else. But I'm sure she didn't get a bad grade because she doesn't do that. Although, that would make her very upset, too." Shelia's thoughts were all over the place.

"Well, let's not speculate, Sheila. You know Maddie. When she's ready to talk, she'll let us—or at least you—know."

Maddie was a "daddy's little girl" but rarely talked to him about the woes of a young woman's life. She wanted him only to think the best of her and didn't want him to know when she struggled through life's ups and downs.

She and her mother were very close, but it was a very different relationship. She was able to share what she was going through, as though Sheila were one of her best friends. Sheila could often give good advice, but more often than not, she struggled with the right things to say to make Maddie feel better. But while Sheila didn't realize it, she actually helped Maddie much more than she could imagine.

"I hope so," Sheila sighed. "I just wish I knew what is wrong so that I, at least, could be a little prepared."

Sheila quickly changed the subject. "But enough about that for now. How did your meeting with the headhunter go?"

"Not as well as I would have liked, but she seems to be very accomplished for her age and already has a lot of great contacts. She warned me, too, that companies aren't hiring as much as they are laying off right now. That just totally caught me off guard. I don't understand why. Business isn't bad right now."

"So you thought," Sheila replied.

"How was your day?" Jake always took an interest in his wife's daily life.

"Pretty uneventful." She paused, then suddenly remembered, "Hey! Don't forget that Duncan has his first flag football game on Saturday. And you promised you'd leave work early on Friday to take him to practice. You won't have to leave work now, obviously, but does that still work for you?"

"Yes. I certainly won't have anything else to do."

Jake and Sheila sat in silence for a couple of minutes as Jake checked his email on his phone. "I'm going upstairs to the office for a bit to make some more calls and send a few emails."

When Jake got upstairs, he knocked softly on Maddie's door. "How was school today, kiddo?"

Maddie shot a quick "fine" in her father's direction.

"Hey! That's not a very nice way to greet your dad. Everything OK?"

"I'm just tired," Maddie excused, rolling over onto her other side to face away from her dad on her bed.

"Maybe too many long phone calls and movies on a school night?"

"No, Dad. It has nothing to do with that. Can't I just be tired after school without having a good reason?"

"I suppose you can. I'll leave you alone then. Maybe you can get to bed early tonight."

With the family spread out across the house, they were all very quiet while taking care of their own business. Sheila enjoyed the quiet for a while, but then decided, "It's too quiet in here."

She turned on some music on her phone and switched on her little Bluetooth speaker. Music always calmed her nerves.

At 6:30, Sheila called her family down to dinner. Of course, Duncan was the first to arrive; Maddie was the last. As they sat down, Duncan quickly took over the family ritual of sharing details about their days. He had shared his excitement with Sheila after he got home but had been forced to hold off on sharing it with Jake.

"My coach is so cool, Dad! I can't wait for you to meet him. He played at Ohio State!"

"That's great, Duncan. I hope he's as good a coach as he was a player."

"And, Dad!" Duncan was speed-talking with his volume on high. "Don't forget about my football practice on Friday. You promised you'd take me."

"I can't wait," Jake told him, and he really couldn't. He loved watching Duncan play sports, and even though it would only be a practice, it would be a nice distraction. Then, with the actual game on Saturday, he had a few things to look forward to enjoying.

"Maddie, you haven't said a word. And you really don't look like you're eating, despite how much you are pushing your food around. How was your day?" Jake tried again to engage his daughter.

"I told you earlier that it was fine, Dad," Maddie grumbled. For once, she had been grateful that Duncan was rambling on and dominating the dinner conversation.

"OK." Jake quickly looked at Sheila. This was not an issue to deal with at the dinner table in front of Duncan.

The four of them finished dinner, Duncan barely pausing to take a breath while alternating between the topics of football and basketball and the others half-listening as they quietly worried about the issues causing them angst.

After they had eaten and the kids had cleaned up and returned to their bedrooms to finish their homework, Sheila decided to check on Maddie. She took a deep breath and peeked in the door.

"Maddie, do you have a second?"

"Yeah," Maddie whispered and closed her book.

"You say everything is fine, but you don't seem like it. What's going on?"

Maddie wasn't ready to talk to her mom about what she had witnessed at the coffee shop that afternoon. She didn't know how to tell her mom and wanted to prepare very carefully ahead of time what she'd say. Instead, she just gave her mom the same answer she gave her dad, "I'm just tired, Mom. I'm going to finish my homework and go to bed early."

Sheila didn't believe Maddie, but she also didn't want to push or pressure her. "OK, sweetie. That sounds like a great idea. Come say goodnight before you go to bed. I love you."

"I love you, too, Mom," Maddie choked back tears, hoping her mom didn't notice.

9

Sheila jumped out of bed the next morning, feeling a little refreshed. She and Jake were both exhausted and went to bed very early the night before. Jake wanted to sleep away some stress, and since Sheila hadn't slept a wink the night before, she was ready for bed before she even got up that day.

That morning proceeded much like the day before, but Sheila didn't have to drive the kids to school, so she sat down to watch a little news and enjoy a second cup of coffee before her 9:30 spin class.

Just as she sat down and grabbed the remote, the phone rang. She almost didn't answer because the only calls that seemed to come in on the hard line were robocalls or other telemarketing calls. She went ahead and looked at the caller ID and noticed that it was the Imaging office where she had her mammogram the day before. Sheila expected a quick chat, as someone would tell her everything looked fine with her images.

"Mrs. Trestin, this is Marjorie with Highland Imaging Services. How are you this morning?"

"I'm fine, thanks. How about you?"

"I'm fine—The radiologist would like you to come back for some more images. I'm sure there's nothing to be concerned about right now. This is not uncommon. A lot of times doctors need to get a little better look when something shows up a little funny."

"Oh, sure. Yeah, I know what you mean. I've had to have extra shots taken in the past for what turned out to be a normal node that just showed up with a shadow or something. How soon can you get me in?"

"The radiologist would actually like you to come as soon as possible. Is there any chance you can come at 10:00 today? We just had a cancellation."

"Wow! That's quick. I guess I'll be missing my spin class again today, but I can make it at 10:00. Thanks. I'll see you then."

Sheila wasn't too worried after hanging up. As she explained, she knew it wasn't unusual for women to need more images taken after a mammogram. She was actually just more irritated that she had to miss her workout for the second day in a row. A good, hard spin class was exactly what she needed to burn off some stress. "I guess I'll try again tomorrow," she told herself.

Sheila finished her last swallow of coffee and went upstairs to get ready. She wasn't in a hurry, as she had plenty of time to shower and get dressed, but she decided not to call Jake to tell him about her follow-up appointment.

"There's no need to bother Jake with this. He already has enough to worry about. AND I'm sure this is nothing to worry about," she said aloud to herself. She really wasn't too worried, but that little bit of doubt was still creeping into her mind.

10

Shelia sat in the waiting room reading a magazine after her mammogram, waiting for the radiologist to look at the images. There was no sense in going home until she was given the go-ahead. She certainly didn't need to make a third trip.

The technician walked out. "Mrs. Trestin, the radiologist would like me to get some ultrasound pictures. Do you have time to do that now?"

"Oh! Really?" This surprised Sheila. She was sure she would be cleared to go home. "OK. Is there a problem?"

"There's just a spot she still can't see very clearly. It actually looks like it might be a lymph node more under the arm than in the breast tissue. It shouldn't take much time at all if you'd like to come back now."

The ultrasound was over in no time, and Sheila was back in the waiting room when the radiologist came out to speak to her. "Mrs. Trestin, I'm Dr. Juno. It's nice to meet you. Will you please come back to my office?"

Sheila's heart dropped, she could have sworn, all the way down into her stomach. She couldn't even speak; she just stood up and followed the doctor to her office.

At home an hour later, Sheila sat on the sofa, staring straight ahead. She couldn't believe this was happening to her, and she couldn't believe it was happening now. Of course, would there ever be a good time to find out you might have cancer? Dr. Juno had explained what she saw and what she was concerned about, but really, Sheila was in a fog while she explained it. All she could focus on was that she had an appointment with an oncologist in two weeks.

"Really? Two weeks?" she complained to herself. "They tell you that you might have cancer, then there's two weeks of angst and concern before you can see a specialist!"

As she continued to sit in a daze, Sheila decided not to tell Jake right away about what was going on. Under normal circumstances, she didn't hide anything from him, but she wanted to hold off on this news for a little bit. Her appointment was 2 weeks away, and she would tell him before then so that he could go with her, but she'd wait until the time got a little closer.

Maybe Jake would be in a better place with his job search by then. One thing was for sure: She needed Jake with her at the appointment in case the news was really bad. She needed him for support but also for that extra set of ears, as she had proven to herself today her lack of ability to focus on the details of bad news.

Just after she had made that decision, she was startled by a sound behind her. "Jake! I didn't hear you come in! How long have you been standing there?"

"Long enough that you should have known it. Didn't you hear me talking to you?" Jake looked at Sheila suspiciously. "Where were you?"

"I've been right here."

"No," Jake laughed. "Where was your mind? You must have been in deep thought. A nice daydream, I hope."

"Well, you know, we certainly have a lot to think about right now." She knew Jake had no idea just how much there was to think about.

Jake quickly changed the subject. "I'm glad you're here, and I hope you're hungry. I know it's getting late for lunch, but it was my turn to surprise you with lunch. I brought *your* favorite this time—Greek salad with grilled salmon."

"Thank you!" Sheila decided to bottle up her worry for a while and focus on enjoying some more time with her husband. "I could get used to this," she said, with a peck on his cheek.

11

Maddie was dragging through the morning, still upset about her father, when Eli came up from behind her in the hallway. She jumped when she heard him say her name because she was lost in her thoughts of her parents' inevitable divorce and a broken family.

"I tried to call you last night. Did you have a bunch of homework or something?" He flashed her that gorgeous smile.

"I'm sorry, Eli. I did have a lot to do last night. That and some family drama," she paused. The last thing she was going to do was tell Eli that her father was having an affair. "You know how that goes! But all is good now."

"As long as you don't say you were busy with another guy," he laughed. "Let's each lunch together today, unless you have other plans, of course. I don't want to be presumptuous."

"I would love that." Maddie couldn't help the huge grin spreading across her face.

"Great! I'll see you at 12:30 in front of the cafeteria. Oh! Ask Gabby to join us, too, and I'll grab a few guys."

The excitement Maddie felt was enough to put her other worries out of her mind for a while. Nothing was going to ruin this lunch with Eli. As upset and worried as she was about her father and the pretty blonde, she couldn't believe Eli was interested in *her*, and she was only going to think about that for now. She went from sulking through class to floating on air.

"What has happened to you?" Gabby asked when she saw Maddie in Spanish class. "The last time I saw you, just an hour ago, you looked like it was the end of the world. Why this switch?" Gabby guessed and hoped she knew the correct answer. "Eli?"

"Yes! I can't believe this, Gabby. *We* are having lunch with Eli and some of his friends today. We're supposed to meet them at 12:30 in front of the cafeteria, and for now, at least, I don't care about anything but that."

Gabby was nearly as excited as Maddie. After all, Eli had some very cute friends. The girls both had a hard time focusing in class as they both sat daydreaming, not only about lunch that day but also about the fun times ahead. They quickly envisioned dates, parties, and all kinds of fun with the older boys.

It seemed like forever to Maddie and Gabby, but it was actually only two class periods before they were sitting in the cafeteria with Eli, Michael, and their friend Jorge. Everyone was laughing and having a good time when Michael suddenly excused himself. He had someone else he wanted to talk to before the lunch period was over. Then it was just the four of them, Maddie, Gabby, Eli, and Jorge, for 10 more minutes before the next class.

Eli cleared his throat, then asked, "Would you two like to go to a movie with Jorge and me on Sunday afternoon? I mean, I hope you will both come to our game on Friday night, then we have some other plans on Saturday, but we thought it would be fun to catch a movie on Sunday. We'll let you pick the movie."

"Oh! Wow! We'd love that," Maddie quickly answered. "I mean, I guess I shouldn't speak for Gabby. What do you think, Gabby?"

Gabby was totally surprised by the invitation, and her mind felt like it was filled with nothing but gobbledygook. Finally, she managed an answer: "Yeah. That would be cool. I have a research paper due on Monday, but I think I can crank through it before then—now that I have a reason to."

Jorge, who was more reserved than his two friends and even seemed a little shy, smiled, his face turning just a hint of pink. "I'm so glad you can go, Gabby."

"Great! We'll work out the details a little later. We better get to class," Eli again took charge of the conversation. "Maddie, I'll give you a call tonight after practice. In the meantime, maybe you and Gabby can look at the movie listings."

Maddie and Gabby could barely contain their excitement for the rest of the day. They didn't have any more classes together that day, so they were forced to hold their emotions in until they could reconnect at the end of the day. "Come on, Gabby. Let's go get the coffee we didn't get yesterday," Maddie implored, running up to Gabby after school was over.

"I can't, Maddie. Remember, I have piano practice. I have to get home right away."

"Oh yeah. Well, call me as soon as it's over. I'll go home and start looking at movie options."

"Sounds good. Talk later."

Maddie's excitement stuck with her until she walked through the front door of the house. Sheila was on her laptop looking at something, but she quickly closed out of it and slammed the laptop shut when she heard Maddie come in.

"What's up, kiddo? How was your day?"

"It was really good, Mom." But Maddie's joy from just minutes ago had quickly plunged upon seeing her mom, which quickly brought her back to the previous afternoon when she had discovered her father's infidelity. "I'll tell you all about it a little later, but I have some things I need to run upstairs to do."

"I'll talk to you later then. But, Maddie, for someone who had a 'really good' day, you seem a little down again."

"No. No. I promise, Mom. Everything is fine." Maddie couldn't look Sheila in the eye as she said this, so she hoped her mom didn't notice. Of course, Sheila noticed.

When Maddie got upstairs, she quickly grabbed the landline phone from her parents' room. She had come up with an idea on her way home from school because she really needed to figure out what was going on with her dad. She had decided to call him at work, anonymously, to see whether he was in the office that day.

She knew his assistant would answer, so she could pretend to be someone else when asking for him. If she was transferred to her dad, she could just hang up. No one would know it was her because she was calling from the home phone, which was unlisted and wouldn't show up on caller ID.

Maddie dialed the phone, but when she dialed the extension to her dad's office, she was quickly bounced to the main operator. "Oh, hi," Maddie said. "I am looking for Jake Trestin."

Maddie got an answer she didn't expect, which made her a little lightheaded: "I'm sorry, but Mr. Trestin doesn't work here anymore. Is there someone else you would like to speak with instead?"

"No," Maddie paused. "Thanks anyway."

What on earth was going on? Nothing was making sense anymore. Her dad was with another woman, and now her dad was not working? Maddie finally decided she would have to bite the bullet and talk to her dad that evening after dinner. Something was definitely going on, and she didn't want anything interfering with her happiness right now, not with everything going so well with Eli.

12

"Hi, sweetheart," Jake quietly opened the door from the garage. "Are the kids both home?"

"Just in time for dinner. Are you ready to eat? Should I call the kids down? Yes, they are both here, to answer your question."

Sheila smiled at Jake. She didn't want him to know how nervous she was about his job hunting and about her own medical uncertainty. She didn't even ask about his job search that day because she knew if he had something to share, he would tell her. She didn't want to add any extra pressure by constantly asking him about it.

"I'll go get the kids. I'm starving, and I could certainly use a little family time to distract me. Things didn't go any better today than they did yesterday."

"Ugh. I'm sorry but don't worry. I guess we were a little unrealistic to think you could just turn around and find a new job in a day or two. These things take time."

The family was soon seated and chatting about their days. Jake, Sheila, and Maddie were all hiding their own secrets, but they had each decided not to let it show at dinner.

"My turn to share something good!" Duncan exclaimed. "Three more days until my first flag football game!" The rest of the family laughed.

"We know that, Duncan. That isn't something new to share," Maddie chided him, shaking her head and giving him a light shove on the arm.

"It's not new, but it's all that matters to me right now. Do you have something better to share?"

"Actually, I do." Maddie's huge grin from earlier in the day returned to her face. "Eli and his friend Jorge asked Gabby and me to a movie on Sunday. May I go? PLEASE!" Maddie looked back and forth between her mom and dad.

"Well, what are you seeing? How are you getting there? Do you have any details?" Jake inquired.

"I don't know any of that yet. Eli and I are talking later. The guys told Gabby and me to pick the movie."

"Eli seemed very nice when he was here. I think it would be fine for you to go, as long as you get your homework done. In case you have forgotten, Duncan's first game is Saturday," Sheila chimed in, stone-faced.

Duncan rolled his eyes at his mom's joke, but Jake and Maddie found the humor in it.

"Seriously, though, you need to go watch your brother play, and I'm sure you're also planning to go to the football game on Friday night."

"I know. I'm going to work a little extra every night to get ahead. I'm definitely going to the game on Friday night. I don't want to miss anything in case Eli does something great, and I'm sure he will. I guess Gabby and I need to figure out what position Jorge plays so that we can watch for him, too."

"He's a wide receiver," Duncan quickly told his sister.

"Duncan! How do you know so much? You don't even go to the high school."

"I know ALL."

"Oh boy!" It was Maddie's turn to roll her eyes.

Maddie and Duncan quickly filled the dishwasher after dinner. Duncan had his usual plans of rushing through his homework so that he could move on to gaming. Maddie, on the other hand, had a full slate: finishing extra homework, talking to Gabby about the weekend and the boys, talking to Eli, and having the dreaded conversation with her dad.

Maddie went up to her room to start her homework but couldn't concentrate with so many conflicting emotions running through her. She darted off a quick text: "Pls come 2 my rm."

Just a minute later, Jake walked in. "What's up?" he asked enthusiastically, remembering Maddie's mood from the night before.

"Oh, Dad," Maddie immediately broke down crying. She hadn't expected this reaction on seeing her dad come into her room, but she had always thought him to be almost perfect. She just didn't understand what was going on with him.

"Hey, hey, hey. It's OK, honey. What's wrong?"

"Saw you—coffee—called—home early—" Maddie really couldn't make much sense with her explanation, or at least, Jake couldn't make much sense of what she was saying through her sobs.

Jake grabbed a couple of tissues from Maddie's nightstand. "Here. Blow your nose, take a few breaths, and try again to tell me what's going on."

"I saw you yesterday at the coffee shop, Dad. You were with some young, hot blonde woman. And you've been home from work early every day this week. I called you at work today, and they told me you don't work there anymore," Maddie said it all quickly without a breath, before she could break down again.

Jake let out a heavy sigh. "Let's grab Duncan and go downstairs with your mom."

Sheila again slammed the laptop shut as the other three entered the room. A much different mood hung over them as they all sat around the sofas in the family room. Duncan and Maddie both looked blankly back and forth between their parents.

Jake cleared his throat. "I have something to tell you, which I was hoping I wouldn't have to tell you at all, at least not until I had better news to share."

Jake wanted to sound calm and confident so that his kids didn't worry. "I lost my job. I just found out on Monday, and I've spent the last few days putting out feelers and meeting with people, trying to find a new opportunity. That's who you saw me with yesterday, Maddie, a headhunter. I didn't tell you guys right away because I didn't want to worry you. I was hoping to find something new quickly, then tell you that I had a new job."

"We're sorry, Dad. That really sucks," Duncan said with compassion.

"Yeah, kiddo, it does suck, as you state so eloquently," Jake chuckled.

"Oh, Dad. I feel so awful. I was so mad at you because I knew something was going on that you weren't telling us. I should have trusted you and just asked you right away."

"Is this what's been bothering you, Maddie?" Sheila asked. "I thought something had happened at school. You were so down last night and didn't seem to be yourself again this afternoon right after school."

"My emotions have definitely been on a roller coaster," Maddie giggled. "I'm glad to know the truth, Dad. You should have just told us; we aren't little kids anymore. And besides, you are Super Dad! You'll figure out something soon."

"Yeah, I'm not worried either," Duncan also assured his dad.

And with that, Maddie and Duncan both gave Jake a quick hug and raced back up to their rooms to continue with their evening rituals.

"I'm glad *they* are so confident. I wish I had as much faith in this process as they do," Jake sighed.

Sheila didn't say anything; instead, she just reached over, grabbed her husband's hand, and gave it a squeeze.

13

Duncan felt like he was on top of the world when he woke up on Saturday morning. Practice the night before couldn't have been better. He had rushed home from school, eaten a healthy snack, and dressed for practice 2 hours before it was time to go. The best thing of all was that his dad was there to take him to practice.

And things could not have gone better once he was there. For all the times he had heard he should work harder on his schoolwork, he made up for it on the field. He ran harder and faster, took fewer breaks, and just did everything a step or two above everyone else.

As a wide receiver, he enjoyed 'juking' those trying to cover him. (That was the term he and Jake had adopted to describe how he could quickly change direction and fool the defense.) As a defensive back, he knew exactly the right angle to take to cut off the offensive player carrying the ball.

Things had gone so well at practice that several of the other parents had approached Jake to talk about Duncan and ask whether he had played before.

"How long has he been playing football?

"What other sports does he play?

"Did he get those skills from you?"

Jake loved hearing these questions and talking about Duncan almost as much as Duncan loved hearing about it later. Jake had been a good athlete in high school, but his skills couldn't measure up to those of his son. Jake could already tell, even at Duncan's young and inexperienced age, that he had something natural that couldn't be taught and most kids never grew into.

Sheila made sure to make Duncan a protein-packed breakfast—egg, bacon, and cheese sandwich—but he didn't even finish half of it.

"Duncan, please. You need to eat more," Sheila pleaded with him.

"I can't, Mom. You know I can't eat that much in the morning, and I'm just too psyched for my first game."

"I know, but—"

"We'll take it with us. I promise I'll eat more of it at halftime."

The entire family was soon in the car, and Duncan sat quietly and didn't participate in any of the chitchat around him. He felt like he was in a zone and didn't want to be snapped out of it. Before he knew it, he was on the field, and the game was starting.

Duncan felt like he was playing against younger kids—his skills were so much more advanced than the other kids around him. His team had won the coin toss and started on offense. The quarterback took no time in getting the ball to Duncan, time after time, though he was very disappointed when at the 10-yard line, the handoff went to the running back, who got to score the first touchdown.

"That's so unfair!" Maddie exclaimed to her parents on the sideline. "Duncan did all the work to get down the field, but someone else got to score."

"It's OK. Football is a team sport. Duncan will get his chance to score," Jake assured her.

And that chance he got, even sooner than expected because when Duncan switched positions from wide receiver to defensive back, he made an interception on the very first pass by the opposing quarterback, and he ran it back for a touchdown. Duncan's first 6 points of the season came while he was playing defense.

And so the game went. Duncan went on to score another 3 touchdowns, those all on offense, along with 2 extra points (they didn't kick extra points at this age, so they ran a play for an extra point), and his team won 34-6. The opposing team only scored one touchdown, and that was when the coach had taken Duncan out to give him a short break and allow someone else a chance to play.

Duncan was ecstatic after the game and ran immediately to his dad. That's when he saw Eli standing with Maddie. "Oh wow! You were here, Eli? I didn't know you were coming?"

"Hey! Congrats, Duncan. You were great. I got here right at the beginning of the second half. I know you came to my game last night, so I figured I owed you the same."

"Thanks! You had a great game last night, too." Duncan was beaming with pride that the high school quarterback had come to watch him play, even if it was because he mostly came to see Maddie.

"Want to come to our house and have pizza with us?" Duncan quickly looked at his sister after inviting Eli.

Eli also looked at Maddie. "Is that OK with you, Maddie?"

"Of course!" Maddie tried not to sound too excited.

"Just let me make a quick call, then I'll be free to come. Want to ride with me, Maddie?"

"Can I come, too?" Duncan jumped in.

"Mom and Dad, may I please ride with Eli?" Maddie knew she had better get permission. She had never ridden in a car with a guy before.

Jake glanced at Eli, then said, "I guess that would be OK." Then at Duncan, "Duncan, you come with Mom and me. I want to talk more about the game." He knew Maddie didn't want her little brother stealing time from Eli, and Jake legitimately wanted to rehash the game with Duncan.

"Awww."

"Maybe next time, Duncan. Come on! I want to hear what you thought about your first game."

That prompt for more was all it took. In fact, that's all Duncan could talk about the rest of the evening. He couldn't believe how great everything was right now. He was the star of his team, and the star of the high school team was now coming to watch him and even to eat dinner at his house.

14

Once every piece of pizza had been eaten and Duncan had gone upstairs to shower, Eli and Maddie went outside to sit on the deck and talk. They had only been sitting on the gliding sofa for about 10 minutes when it started to get very chilly, so Maddie went back inside to ask her father to light the fire pit. She was hoping Eli would be able to stay for a while since it still wasn't that late.

Jake looked at Sheila once Maddie had gone back outside. "She's a little young to be cuddling with some boy on the back deck, isn't she?"

"I think she's fine. He really seems to be a nice boy. I mean, he certainly hasn't been shy about spending time around us, and he hasn't even known Maddie that long. And besides, we are right inside the door from them. I don't think anything fishy is going to happen."

Jake laughed at himself. "I suppose you're right. We can easily see them through the window. I'm just looking out for my little girl."

Once Jake had lit the fire pit and given Eli one quick glance of warning, he went back inside to watch TV with Sheila.

"Your parents are very nice," Eli told Maddie.

"Yeah, they're OK. But I really don't want to talk about my parents, do you?"

Eli laughed, "No, I do not!"

"I thought you had plans today and that's why you asked us to go to the movie tomorrow. What happened? Or do you have somewhere to go from here?"

"Well, once your brother so politely asked me to come over for pizza, I made that quick call to cancel my plans. It's not a big deal. Some of us were just supposed to hang out at Ella's house tonight."

"I think I know who Ella is. She's a junior, too, right?"

"Yeah. She's pretty cool. You should get to know her."

"I'm sorry you canceled your plans. You didn't need to do that for my sake," Maddie apologized. "And you certainly didn't need to do it for Duncan!" She laughed.

"Don't worry," Eli assured her. "I didn't do it for Duncan or even for you." He winked. "I did it for me. This is where I want to be tonight."

Maddie felt a warm feeling rush through her body. It was a feeling she had never felt before. Was it happiness? Disbelief? Or maybe the beginnings of some feelings that went way beyond a crush.

She couldn't believe how easy it was to sit and talk to Eli. Whenever she'd had feelings for a boy in the past, she had sort of clammed up and gotten very shy. So much so that she had a hard time thinking of anything to say. That wasn't happening with Eli.

They talked about their childhoods, school, and their favorite foods. Every subject just seemed to flow so naturally.

"So, what's your favorite kind of music?" Maddie was a music lover and wondered whether Eli shared the same passion.

"I mostly listen to hip hop, like every other kid our age. But my tastes are very broad. I like almost every kind of music." He paused and with a bit of apprehension, he added, "Everything but country music, that is."

"Me, too!" Maddie exclaimed. "And what's your favorite love song?" Maddie blushed and was immediately sorry she asked the second it came out of her mouth. Luckily, the question didn't seem to faze Eli.

"I'll tell you, but you have to promise not to make fun of me."

"I won't. But now I'm definitely curious."

"OK—my favorite love song is an old one: *All Out of Love* by Air Supply." Eli cringed in anticipation of her response. After all, most kids their age had probably never even heard of Air Supply, let alone their sappy hit song from 1980.

"What?" Maddie couldn't help but chuckle a little. "What are you? A 55-year-old woman?" She let out a nervous chuckle, remembering her promise not to tease him.

"No, but my mom is, and now, since you broke your promise and insist on making fun of me, I'm going to make you feel bad. When I was a little baby, my mom used to sing to me. I don't remember that, of course, but apparently it was the only song that would calm me down when she was rocking me. I guess I was colicky or something, whatever that is. Anyway, that song kind of stuck, and she kept singing it to me for many years when she would tuck me in at night. I know it's a weird song to share with my mom, but it has meaning."

Eli had never shared this story with anyone, but he wasn't even embarrassed to share it with Maddie. He was also feeling a comfort that he hadn't shared with other girls.

"Oh, my God! I'm such a jerk! I'm sorry I made fun of you. That's the sweetest story I've ever heard. I just picture little baby Eli in his mom's arms."

"That's OK. I forgive you." He gave her a tiny, light punch on the arm.

"Oh! I can't believe I forgot to ask. Did you and Gabby decide on a movie?"

"Yeah. What about the new one with Kevin Hart and Dwayne Johnson? We figured that would be funny but would also have a lot of action. It should have something for all of us."

"That sounds great. And on that note, I should probably be heading home. It's getting pretty late, and I don't want to make your dad mad at me already."

"Do you think he'll let me pick you up tomorrow? We wouldn't be alone. I could pick up Jorge first, then you, then Gabby."

"Probably, since we'd all be together. And Gabby could actually come over here so that you don't have to pick her up separately."

"Sounds good, but double-check. I'll talk to Jorge to see what time works for him. Does it matter to you and Gabby what time we go?"

"Nope."

Eli glanced inside. As much as he wanted to kiss Maddie, he didn't want to do it with the chance that her parents were watching from inside.

"It's probably best," he told himself. He really liked Maddie and didn't want her to think he was just out for something. He thought the best course of action was to take Maddie inside, thank her parents for the pizza and their hospitality, and ask permission himself to pick up Maddie and Gabby tomorrow. Instead of a kiss, he gave Maddie a quick hug at the front door when he left.

<h1 style="text-align:center">15</h1>

Sheila was surprised to discover that Jake was already up when she woke up on Sunday morning. She took a little time to take a quick shower, brush her teeth, and get dressed before heading downstairs. She figured that since Jake was already downstairs, he would have made himself some coffee.

"Good morning, honey. You're up early today," she greeted Jake when she went down to the kitchen to start making Sunday brunch. Jake was sitting at the kitchen table with the laptop open. "Are you already at the job hunt this morning? I thought you'd give yourself a little break today."

"No time for breaks, Sheila. But is there something you want to tell me?"

Oh, no! Sheila felt a little panic creep in and overcome her. She'd almost been caught several times when searching medical websites and had slammed shut the laptop when people had come up behind her or come in and surprised her. She couldn't believe she must have left open a site.

How could she have been so careless? She stared at Jake with a blank face. "Uhhhh—" was the only thing she could manage. She had planned to tell Jake about her upcoming appointment, but she didn't want to tell him yet and certainly didn't want him to find out this way.

"Are you thinking about going back to work?" Jake questioned her. "You left a site open."

"Oh!" Sheila was relieved. She *had* been thinking about going back to work on a freelance basis for a few months. The kids didn't need her as much anymore, and if she eased back into work, she could still have time to volunteer at school, the women's center, and the hospital. Now that Jake wasn't working, the time couldn't be better.

Obviously, she wasn't happy that Jake lost his job, but it gave her that extra little motivation to investigate what was available. Thankfully, that was the website she had left open.

"Yes. I've actually been thinking about it for a while. I think I'd like to pick up some simple proofreading work first, just to get my feet wet again." Sheila laughed. "I feel like I need to warm up my eyes—and my brain—a little before getting into any intense editing work. What do you think?"

"I think it's great if that's something you really want to do. I'm sorry if my situation is making you think you *have* to find work. Are you sure you really want to do this? I suppose it would help in case my unemployment drags on." Jake rolled his eyes as he thought about the past week.

"Yes, Jake, I'm sure." Sheila gave her husband a quick squeeze and a peck on the cheek. "As I said, I've been thinking about it for a while, months actually. I guess I should thank you for giving me that extra incentive I needed."

"Ha! Yeah, right. I'm glad I could help with that."

"And on that note, want to help me make brunch?" Sheila asked as she poured a cup of coffee. "I thought we'd make waffles for Maddie, bacon for Duncan, and eggs and fruit salad."

"Sure. Let's do it."

As Sheila and Jake moved around the kitchen, both were taken back about 20 years when they were dating. They would make brunch together about every weekend; he made the scrambled eggs while she made everything else. He would set the table and pour them each some juice while she finished what she was making. They were young then and hadn't yet started drinking morning coffee. These days coffee in the morning was a must.

"Remember when we used to do this together all the time, Sheila?" Jake looked lovingly at his wife.

"I was just thinking the same thing!" Sheila again walked over and wrapped her arms around him. He returned the hug, and they stood that way for about 30 seconds when suddenly Duncan came bounding down the stairs and into the kitchen.

"Smells great, Mom! Bacon!"

"Yes. And you can thank your father for helping with brunch today. He made the eggs."

"Can we eat now? I'm starving."

"Be patient. It's almost ready. Why don't you run back up and get your sister," Jake asked, "then it will be ready."

They had just finished eating when Maddie's phone rang in the other room. Her head jerked up. "May I please go see who it is? Remember, we have plans to see a movie today, and we need to finalize our plans."

"Go ahead," Jake told her. "But please come back to help clean up when you are done."

Maddie was halfway to her phone before Jake finished his first two words. She was thrilled to see that it was Eli calling. Actually, she was pretty sure it was Eli, since she had talked to Gabby as soon as she woke up. She had texted Gabby quickly the night before to tell her she'd had a 'perfect day' but waited until morning to call her with all the details.

"Did he kiss you?" had been Gabby's first question.

"No, but I was really hoping he would." Maddie sighed. "I suppose it would have been weird and awkward, though, since Mom and Dad were right inside and probably could have seen us."

"Yeah, I suppose. But it was dark out."

"It's fine, Gabby. It really was the perfect day." And as much as Maddie had wanted Eli to kiss her, she was also very nervous about it. If and when he did, it would be Maddie's first real kiss. She'd had the awkward, rushed, Dorito-tainted kisses during games of spin the bottle in seventh grade, but she barely even considered those as kisses.

"How about a 1:50 movie? Did Gabby get her paper done?" Eli asked after Maddie's "Hello?"

"I talked to Gabby this morning, and she said any time works for her. What time do you want to pick us up? I'll make sure she is here before then."

"Well," Eli thought, "I'll get Jorge first, about 1:00, I guess, then I'll head over there. That should be more than enough time to get there and get a snack. And actually, I'll get the tickets online as soon as we hang up. That will save us time and make sure we get good seats." They were going to the theater with reserved seating, and all the good seats sold out pretty quickly on weekends.

"Sounds great." Maddie tried to show only an appropriate amount of excitement. "And meanwhile, I'll run these plans past my parents."

"OK, text me and tell me what they say."

"Sounds good. Bye."

"Later, Maddie. See you soon."

"Can't wait," Maddie said to herself dreamily after she had hung up.

16

Jake and Sheila signed off on the plans pretty quickly. After all, the theater was only about 5 minutes away, and they already felt pretty good about Eli. He seemed to be a very nice and polite kid. Sheila even called Claire to explain the situation and give her approval, since Claire didn't know Eli nor Jorge. "Our little babies are growing up," Claire had sighed.

Claire went in to say hi when she dropped off Gabby a little before 1:00. After a quick greeting and hugs for everyone in the Trestin family, she was about to head out when Sheila told her to stay to meet the boys.

"We don't have anything going on today, anyway. You can stick around for a bit if you want." Sheila was actually hoping to have some alone time with Claire. She'd told her about Jake losing his job, but she hadn't yet told her about her medical scare. And it would be fun to talk about the kids once they were gone!

Just about then, the doorbell rang, and the girls ran to the front door.

"Is it OK if we come in and say hi to your parents, Maddie? We want to make a good impression," Eli explained.

They all laughed.

"And my mom is here, too," Gabby warned them. "Don't worry; she's really cool."

After a few pleasantries and a couple of minutes of small talk, they were soon in Eli's car and on the way to the movie. Eli and Maddie did their best to do most of the talking and ask questions, since Gabby and Jorge didn't really know each other. Maddie remembered all too well how intimidating that could be, and she really wanted Gabby and Jorge to hit it off.

With the kids gone, Sheila asked Claire into the kitchen for a glass of iced tea.

At that, Jake called Duncan downstairs. "Hey, kiddo, want to head to the mall to find a pair of basketball sneakers? We might as well get a pair now while I have the time, even though tryouts aren't for a couple more weeks."

"Yes! Awesome, Dad. Thanks."

Jake knew that the kids and their activities had often taken a backseat to his work schedule, and he was excited to make up for it in any way he could while he could. In years past, Sheila would have been the one taking him for shoes. Now, he was probably just as excited for this outing as Duncan was.

Sheila and Claire now had the house to themselves, and Sheila let it all out. A few tears sneaked out, but she held her composure pretty well. All the stress of the week just needed to come out. First the job loss, then the mammograms, ultrasound, and news about her oncology appointment, and now Jake discovered that she was thinking about returning to work.

"Now I feel like I really *need* to do it. It's not that I don't want to find work, but what if I get bad news from the doctor? And on top of everything, I'll need to find clients. I was excited when I wanted to work again, but now there's a lot of extra pressure."

Sheila was always so strong in front of her family, but she knew she could let loose with Claire, and she knew Claire would have exactly the right thing to say. In this case, it wasn't so much what Claire said, but her calmness and reassurance alone helped. She simply grabbed Sheila's hand and held it tight.

"You know we'll all get through this together, Sheila."

And Sheila knew she was right. With just that simple gesture and those few words, Sheila felt comforted.

"Now let's change the subject and talk about those boys!" Sheila quickly changed her tone.

"How cute are they?" laughed Claire. "I hope they are as nice as they are cute."

And at the movie, the boys were being very nice. They had treated the girls to popcorn and drinks and were settled in their seats for the previews.

"I love watching the previews," Gabby said. "I'm glad we made it in time."

"Me, too," Jorge smiled at Gabby. "I hate when people walk in front of me or talk during the previews."

As they settled in for the next couple of hours, Maddie's heart leaped when Eli reached over and took her hand. She actually felt her hand tingle and heat rush up her arm. She didn't even mind that she had to reach over with her opposite hand to awkwardly reach the popcorn that sat between the two of them.

Maddie dreaded the movie coming to an end. She really had had the perfect weekend, and she didn't want the day with Eli to end, so she was relieved when the boys asked whether they'd like to get an early dinner together.

"Nothing fancy. Maybe just burgers," Jorge suggested.

"OK. But only if you let us pay this time. You guys have paid for everything," Maddie insisted and Gabby agreed.

Seated at the booth in the burger place next door, Maddie wasn't very hungry. She had eaten too much popcorn. But she didn't want Eli to think she was one of those girls who was afraid to eat in front of a boy, and besides, she knew she'd need to eat sometime, and a burger sounded really good.

"OK. You guys, please don't think I'm weird, but Gabby, do you want to split a burger and fries with me? I ate way too much popcorn." Maddie blushed.

"Great idea. So did I. And since we are eating pretty early, which is no problem at all, I'm not too hungry either." Gabby didn't want them to think she was complaining.

Now that they weren't in a hushed movie theater, they all had more of a chance to talk and get to know each other. They talked about gossip coming out of the first weeks of school, about the football game on Friday night, and about their families, which is where Maddie became a little more reserved. She didn't want to slip and let Eli and Jorge know that her father had just lost his job. She knew that it shouldn't be, but for some reason, it was a little embarrassing for Maddie.

After the girls had paid and they were all walking back to the car, Eli suggested that he first drop off Jorge, then

Gabby, then Maddie. Maddie felt that rush of adrenaline again, knowing that she'd have a little alone time with Eli.

Jorge had an awkward goodbye, as he and Gabby weren't quite sure what, if anything, was going on with them yet. And as soon as he got out of the car, the questions started flying at Gabby.

"Guys, come on. Jorge is super nice, but let's just see. I can't tell you much yet." But inside, Gabby knew something was there. She was feeling some of the same emotions that Maddie had described to her.

Gabby climbed out of the car 10 minutes later, and finally, Eli and Maddie were alone.

"Today was super fun, Maddie."

"I had a great time, too. The entire weekend was great. I wish it didn't have to end now."

"I know, but I guess it does. I heard you tell your mom you'd be home by 7:00, and it's getting pretty close."

"Yeah. Dinner wasn't part of the original deal, so I need to get inside and finish up my homework. I'm basically done, but I have to study for a quiz tomorrow."

A light drizzle had become an unseasonable snow flurry when Eli pulled into the Trestin's driveway. They had both climbed out of the car when Eli called, "Maddie, wait." He walked over to where she stood, out of sight of the front windows and door, and grabbed both of her hands, and pulled her close to him.

Maddie hardly had time to register what was happening when, there in the light snowfall, Eli leaned down and kissed her very softly.

17

Sheila sat hand-in-hand with Jake in the oncologist's office, waiting for her to come speak with them. Dr. Beckham was supposed to be the best in the Chicago area. Once Sheila had told Jake about her mammograms, ultrasound, and upcoming doctor's appointment, he redid much of the research that Sheila had already done. He was relieved to learn that they were in the care of the best oncologist in Chicago, perhaps even one of the best in the country.

Sheila had put on a brave face when she called him to the sofa to sit beside her once the kids had gone upstairs after dinner one evening. Jake kept that same brave face as she explained the entire situation.

"Oh, Sheila. I can't believe you've kept this bottled up inside. I wish you would have told me," Jake had soothed her.

"Well, you've had enough to deal with right now. I didn't want to burden you with one more thing until I had to, and besides, that's what best friends are for. I dumped it all on Claire one day."

"I'm glad Claire was there for you, but I hope you know after all of these years that you are *never* a burden to me."

Sheila and Jake were both thinking back to this exchange when the office door suddenly opened. While they had both done a lot of research on the doctor, they couldn't believe how young she actually looked when she came in. Jake dropped Sheila's hand and reached up and put his arm around her shoulder after they had all done introductions and as Dr. Beckham sat down behind her desk.

Dr. Beckham quickly got down to business. She explained that she did not want to jump to any conclusions and make a diagnosis until Sheila had some more tests done, so when they were done talking, Sheila would next move to a procedure room to have blood drawn and a biopsy done. Based on the results of the bloodwork and biopsy, Sheila might have to return for more tests.

"It sounds as though there's something you aren't telling us, Dr. Beckham. It sounds to me like you're expecting some bad news if you are already looking down the road to other tests," Jake questioned without asking an actual question.

"Look, I don't want either of you to worry until we know something for sure, but I fear some type of lymphoma. That's just a possibility. We'll get the results of the biopsy back in a couple of days, then we can go from there. We have an excellent pathologist in our practice, and he'll be working with me on your diagnosis. In the meantime, please try to be positive and don't get too frustrated."

"Easy for you to say," Sheila groaned with a forced grin.

"I know, but I've seen many cases in which people literally make themselves sick with worry, and it was all for naught." Dr. Beckham took a few seconds to give a reassuring look and a smile. "Now, let's get you next door for those tests. Mr. Trestin, if you don't mind heading out to the waiting room, it shouldn't take too long."

Sheila and Jake were both in a daze following the biopsy, and they seemed to stay that way for the next few days. They both went through the regular motions of their new daily lives, but their minds were often far off in thought.

They had decided again to keep yet another secret from the kids. But this secret definitely made sense. Just as Sheila had spared Jake the worry for several days, they wanted to do the same for Maddie and Duncan.

But Maddie and Duncan weren't as clueless as their parents had hoped. It was hard not to notice that both of their parents often seemed distracted. They had talked and decided that Jake and Sheila were probably worried about Jake finding a job.

The ringing phone snapped Sheila and Jake out of a daze at 9:00 one morning. It had been 3 days since the biopsy, so they both looked at each other immediately.

"Do you think—?" Sheila's voice trailed off.

"Well, let's find out," Jake answered and handed the phone to Sheila as he sneaked a look at the caller ID.

"Hello?—Hi, Dr. Beckham—OK—Uh-huh." Sheila let out a heavy sigh. "What is Hodgkin's lymphoma versus non-Hodgkin's lymphoma—What's my prognosis—I can come in for tests about any time, well, preferably during the school day so that our kids aren't around—tomorrow at 10:00—OK—Thank you, Dr. Beckham. I'll see you tomorrow."

Jake had felt all the blood leave his face and felt weak in the legs as he listened to his wife speak. He had to sit down and wondered how Sheila was keeping her composure.

"Well, at least now we know," Sheila managed a little smile, but her entire body was shaking.

"What exactly do we know?" Jake felt totally numb and was surprised he could even speak, though with a raspy voice.

"Lymphoma. We have to go back tomorrow for a CT scan and a bone marrow biopsy. She said something about Reed-Sternberg cells, which means Hodgkin's lymphoma, I believe." Sheila's voice finally broke as she finished her thought, and the tears started streaming down her face.

"Let's go to the sofa." Jake wrapped his arm around her and guided her to the other room. There they sat while Jake held his wife and she wept on his lap. He told himself to be strong, but soon tears were rushing down his face, as well. Nothing else mattered anymore—not his job, not money. Everything was about his family right now and the health of his wife. "We'll get through this," he assured her. He felt as though that had been an all-too-common reassurance lately.

18

The next several days passed very slowly. Sheila had gotten through the next round of tests without the kids suspecting anything, so they thought. She and Jake had decided to keep the news from them for a little longer until they had some more definitive answers. They had just returned from their latest appointment with Dr. Beckham when Maddie and Duncan walked into the house after school.

"Can you both come into the family room?" Jake called out.

"What's up?" Duncan was the first to ask as he glanced over at his sister. The truth was that Duncan and Maddie had noticed something was up. Their parents had both gone from being in a perpetual daze to showing an overabundance of love and attention. It was confusing to both of them, but they had still decided it was just a weird time. Maybe their parents were getting more concerned about the lack of an income.

"We have some upsetting news to talk to you about," Jake was the first to speak.

"Is it Grandpa?" This concern was always Duncan's first thought when he knew bad news was coming. He was very close to his grandfather, who had suffered some health issues over the past few years.

"No, it's me," Sheila mustered a smile. "Please try not to worry too much. We are all going to keep a positive attitude through this. I *need* you to keep a positive attitude, please."

"What, Mom? You're really scaring us," Maddie pleaded.

Sheila looked at Jake and nodded. She needed him to help explain the situation.

"Mom and I just returned from the doctor's office. Mom has actually been going through some tests over the past few days, a couple of weeks actually."

Duncan and Maddie again looked at each other as everything started to make sense. Both had lost all color in their faces.

"She has been diagnosed with a type of cancer."

"No!" Maddie and Duncan both exclaimed and immediately started crying.

"It's OK. It's OK," Sheila hugged both of them.

"No. It's not OK, Mom. What is it? What does it mean for you?" Maddie sobbed.

"She has what's called Hodgkin's lymphoma, and it's treatable. We are very lucky that they found it when they did. It's Stage 1, which means the cancer is limited to just one area in her body."

"Right here under this arm," Sheila showed them.

"Mom is going to have a tough few months because she has to go through chemotherapy and radiation. While they found it early and it's in the early stage, the doctors want to be very aggressive to make sure they get it all and prevent any reoccurrence."

"What are chemo-whatever-you-said and radiation?" Duncan wondered.

"I'll have to go to the hospital and basically have poison pumped into my body. It sounds awful, but it's what helps kill the cancer. Unfortunately, it might also make me feel very sick, and I could also lose my hair. But, hey! Who wants to take care of hair at a time like this, anyway?" Sheila tried to add a little joke to this heavy news.

"And then I'll get radiation once I'm done with chemo. That means I'll lay on a table and a machine will direct beams at the area to kill cells. This won't make me sick like the chemo."

"When will all of this start?" Duncan asked. "Will you be able to see one more of my games before then?"

"Duncan! Is that all you care about? Your stupid games?" Maddie scolded.

"No, Maddie." Duncan shot Maddie an angry glare. "But I know Mom loves going to my games, and I was worried for her sake that she couldn't go anymore. I mean, this year, while she's sick."

"You're right, Duncan. I do love going to your games, and I'll be there on Saturday. My chemo starts next week, so nothing can keep me from your game this week."

"Good," Duncan sighed.

"And I'm hoping I can still go to your games even after I start chemo. I won't be sick all the time, and maybe I'll even get lucky. Some people don't feel sick."

"Who's going to take care of you, Mom, if you don't feel well?" Maddie asked.

"Well, who am I?" Jake teased. "You don't think I can take care of Mom?"

"Yes, Dad, but I thought you might get a new job and have to leave her alone. Duncan and I have to be at school."

"I certainly do hope to find a job soon, but nothing is more important to me right now than your mother. Plus, do you really think Grammy is going to stay away? I, for one, know that she'll be on the first plane here once she gets this news."

"Now, who's hungry?" Sheila changed the subject. "I know I am." She was actually hungry for the first time in many days. Even with the bad news, she felt a sense of relief that she had shared the news with her kids. "We really *will* get through this together," she told herself.

"I'm hungry!" Duncan chimed in.

"Of course, you are," Maddie rolled her eyes.

"Let's order dinner tonight. I think we all deserve a treat," Sheila told them. "What do you all want?"

"You pick, Mom. I want to get what you want." Right now, Duncan only wanted whatever would make his mom happy.

"Actually, I could go for a good pizza. With extra pepperoni! Forget the healthier veggie pizza for tonight," Sheila laughed.

19

Maddie couldn't answer her phone when Eli called that evening. What was usually her favorite part of the night couldn't distract her from what she was feeling. She had tried to put on a cheerful face for her mom, and she thought she'd done pretty well at hiding her fear, but the truth was that she was scared to death. She was scared of losing her mom, but she was almost equally as scared of what her mother would have to go through over the next several months.

Even if her cancer had been caught early and Sheila's prognosis was good, Maddie knew enough about cancer and chemotherapy to know that her mom was about to go through hell. She was still wrapping her head around all of this and wasn't quite ready to talk to anyone—even Eli. Their relationship was too early for him to see her in such a vulnerable mood, or at least she thought.

As awful as it all was, she needed to get some homework done. She sat down to her History homework with hopes that it would actually distract her from her pain. She didn't get very far when her phone rang again. She saw that it was Gabby this time, but she just stared at it for a few more rings before deciding to pick it up.

"Hi, Gabby."

"Oh, Maddie," Gabby cried on the other end. "Are you OK? I'm so sorry."

"I guess your mom told you the news."

"Yes, your mom called and told her that she and your dad had broken the news to you and Duncan tonight. I didn't know until then, but I guess she had already told my mom a few days ago. It's just awful."

"Yes, it is. My mom seems to be taking it in stride, but I'm sure she was just trying to be brave for me and Duncan." Maddie's voice began to shake, and she let out a little sob as she finished her thought.

"Do you need anything?" Gabby would have done anything to make her best friend feel better right then, but she knew there was nothing much she could do except be there for her.

"Not right now, but I'm sure that's coming. What started out as such a great freshman year is about to come crashing down."

"We'll do what we can to salvage it, Maddie. We have to find ways. And hey, you have Eli. Have you told him yet?"

Maddie sighed. "No. He actually called a little bit ago, but I couldn't bear telling him yet. It's all so fresh, and I'm so scared I'll break down. I don't want him to hear me all blubbery and snotty."

"It might actually be better that he *hears* you all blubbery and snotty than *sees* you all blubbery and snotty. Are you sure you don't want to tell him tonight? God forbid you tell him in person and he sees your ugly cry," Gabby tried to lighten the mood.

Maddie faked a laugh. "I suppose you're right. I guess I'll call him back when we hang up."

"I'm going to go then. Besides, Jorge texted me, and I think he's going to call tonight, too."

"He is? I'm sorry. I've been lost in my own sorrows and didn't even think to ask."

"Maddie, please. You have more important things going on than to be thinking of my love life. Give your mom a giant hug from me. I love you both."

"Love you, too, Gabs. Later."

Gabby had a way of making Maddie feel a little better every time she was going through a rough patch. This time was different, though. If anything, she felt even a bit worse after hanging up. She didn't yet feel like calling Eli, so she set the timer on her phone for 30 minutes and got back to her History homework.

In 30 minutes, when the timer went off, she set it for 15 minutes. She went downstairs to get a glass of water, then sat at her desk staring at nothing for the next 10 minutes. Her timer startled her, and she almost spilled her water. She turned off the timer and noticed that Eli had texted her when she was getting her water.

"Sup?" he had asked.

Maddie decided to get it over with. She took a deep breath and promised herself to hold it together.

"Hey, there," Eli answered. "I was beginning to think you were avoiding me."

"Never. I've just had a lot to deal with today," Maddie eased into the conversation.

"Everything OK?"

"No." Maddie's voice shook again. She paused, and she and Eli started to speak over each other.

"I'm sorry, go ahead," Eli told her.

"Eli, my mom has cancer. I just found out after school. I'm just so scared." Tears streamed down her face, but she was determined not to break down.

Eli sat stunned for a moment. He was expecting her to say that she'd had a bad day at school or that she hadn't done well on a test. He wasn't prepared with an answer to this problem.

"Oh, man. That sucks." Eli was angry with himself as soon as it came out of his mouth. "I mean, I'm so sorry, Maddie. Is she going to be OK?"

"Well, I'm telling myself that she is. And I really believe that she is. They caught the cancer early, but she still has to have chemo and radiation, and it's going to be really rough on her."

"Oh, man." Eli rolled his eyes at himself, wondering why that was the only thing he could say. "That sucks."

"Listen. I don't want to burden you with this right now, Eli. It's a lot to comprehend for me and for you. I just wanted to tell you tonight so that you'd know before I see you tomorrow." Maddie rambled on, "I really need to get my homework done, and it's been very hard to concentrate on it, so I'm going to let you go, and I'll see you at school tomorrow."

"OK. Hang in there. See you tomorrow."

"Goodbye."

"Good night, Maddie."

That hadn't gone nearly as well as Maddie had been hoping. She had never felt that awkward with Eli from the time they met. She couldn't help but feel that this news and conversation had broken the trance in which she and Eli had been. She wouldn't be surprised if their very short-lived relationship was over.

Eli also was not happy with the conversation that had just ended. He was furious with himself that he hadn't been a better comfort to Maddie. He just had been taken by surprise. He'd never had to deal with such heavy news before, and he wasn't quite sure how. He was also afraid that he'd been such a disappointment to Maddie that she wouldn't want anything else to do with him.

After all, what kind of doofus can't find something better to say than, "Oh man, that sucks," when he finds out his girlfriend's mother could be dying. *Girlfriend?* he thought to himself. And at that moment, he knew he couldn't end the evening that way.

Maddie was finally able to get a little homework done. Luckily, she didn't have anything else that was due the next day. She headed to the bathroom to wash her face and brush her teeth. She didn't know how well she'd sleep that night, but she thought she'd crash a little early. She had so many thoughts and feelings swirling through her head that she just wanted to escape them all.

Before going to find her parents to say good night, she glanced at her phone and saw that Eli had texted. "Please look out your window."

He had sent the message 15 minutes ago, so Maddie ran to the window, hoping it wasn't too late. She saw Eli standing in the yard with a bouquet of flowers. She ran down the stairs and out the front door in her pajamas. She ran right into Eli's open arms as the flowers fell to the ground.

"Hey. I'm sorry I was such a loser on the phone. I was just so shocked and didn't know what to say. I'm here for you, Maddie. I know it's about to be the worst time of your life, but I want to make it a little easier. Whatever it takes."

Maddie started to cry. "I was so afraid I'd scared you away."

"Never," Eli promised as he held her.

As Maddie cried in Eli's hug, she wished that she'd thought to bring some tissues outside with her. He was going to see her snotty, ugly cry after all.

20

Eli and Maddie spent another 30 minutes together before they both decided he should probably head home. He'd flown out of the house so quickly that he didn't even have time to explain to his parents where he was going. It had been a long day for both of them, and while Eli still needed to get home to finish his homework, Maddie was exhausted and still wanted to sleep away her worries.

She went inside and found Sheila.

"Look what Eli brought us, Mom." She showed her the flowers.

"Those are beautiful." Sheila grinned at Maddie. "He's a very sweet boy."

"Yes. And he brought two bouquets: one for you and one for me. I'll put one in a vase for you to have on the kitchen table. I'm going to put mine on my bedside table so that I can wake up to them and see them while I'm doing homework and stuff in my room."

"Thanks, sweetheart." Sheila paused. "Honey, I know this is going to be a hard time for you, too, but I want you to concentrate on yourself. I want you to have a good freshman year, and I don't want your schoolwork to suffer.

I have faith that I'm going to be OK. I want you to hold on to that faith, too."

"I promise I will." Maddie walked over and gave her mom a big hug. "If it's OK with you, and if you don't need anything, I'm going upstairs to crash. I'm physically *and* mentally exhausted."

"I'm sure you are. It's been a very emotional day. And, no, I don't need anything. Not yet anyway. I'm sure I'll be needing you a lot in the future, so hold on to that offer."

"I love you, Mom."

"I love you."

"Too," Maddie finished her sentence. It was something Maddie and Sheila had been saying since Maddie was about 4 years old when she thought her mommy should finish a returned 'I love you' with a 'too' at the end.

Maddie went upstairs but decided she should do one more thing before going to bed. She knocked lightly on Duncan's door and opened it slowly. She was surprised to find Duncan was already under his covers with the lights off.

"Early night for you, Dunc?" she asked.

"Yeah. I'm really not in the mood for games tonight. I tried, but I just couldn't get into it."

"I totally understand."

They both remained silent for about 20 seconds as Maddie stood in the doorway. Neither was quite sure what to say.

"Welp, goodnight then. I'll see you in the morning."

"Night, sis," he replied.

Maddie made one more quick stop in the bathroom before climbing into her bed, quite positive she would pass out the second her head hit the pillows, despite all the day's stress. Just as she lay down and turned off the light, her door slowly opened.

"Maddie?"

"Yeah, Dunc?"

"Can I sleep with you?"

"Of course. Come on."

Duncan gently climbed into the other side of the bed. It was something they had both done since they were small children. When one or the other was upset or scared about something, they would sneak into the other one's bed. Even though they would often butt heads, the way most siblings do, they also found a lot of comfort in each other. And especially now, they totally knew what the other one was going through.

"I'm scared, Maddie," Duncan finally confessed.

"I am, too, but we have to be strong and positive for Mom."

"Is she going to die?"

"NO!" Maddie refused to think that way, and she certainly didn't want Duncan to think that way either. "I mean, some people die because of cancer, Duncan, but Mom is *not*. They caught it early. Her odds are great. We just need to be here for her."

"Let's be friends then."

"Of course," Maddie laughed. It's what Duncan would say to her usually after they'd been fighting and he was ready to make up. "The last thing Mom needs is for us to get on her nerves because we are bickering and not getting along."

Before Maddie could even finish the sentence, she heard Duncan breathing heavily behind her and knew that he'd fallen asleep. Cuddled back to back, it didn't take her long to do the same.

21

Duncan woke up on Saturday morning, bound and determined to give his mom a great game that day. He had probably never been as excited for a game because he really wanted to gift his mom with something special before she started treatment that week. He got up early that morning and did something he never did before a game.

"Did you take a shower?" Sheila asked him when he came down for breakfast.

"Yep! I wanted to get my blood going. I'm psyched for my game today," he beamed.

"So am I," she beamed right back and him. "And here, for my superstar football player, is his favorite breakfast."

Jake and Maddie both walked into the kitchen just moments later.

"Duncan! Did you shower? Before going to play a football game?" Jake laughed at him.

"I knew something smelled a little different," Maddie teased. "It's usually a little smelly when I sit down beside you."

"Ha Ha," Duncan replied flatly.

"Just kidding, 'friend'." Maddie elbowed him in the arm.

They managed to sit and have an enjoyable meal together before having to leave 30 minutes later. Most meals since hearing the bad news had had a forced lightness to them. They all had heavy hearts, but no one wanted to burden the others, so they tried to talk about superficial subjects. That morning was different, as they enjoyed a light-hearted and fun meal conversation. Duncan also surprised them for a second time that morning by finishing his entire breakfast.

As they were clearing the table, Duncan asked, "Is Eli going to the game again today, Maddie?"

"Yes, he is. In fact—" Maddie paused to look at her phone. "He just pulled up. He's going to ride with us today. You don't care, right, Dad?"

"Of course not. Tell him we'll be right out."

"OK, thanks, Dad. I'm going out," Maddie hollered as she ran toward the front door.

"Duncan, make your water bottle really quick. I left an empty bottle sitting on the counter," Sheila instructed. "I'm going to grab a sweater."

"And I'll pour us coffees to go," Jake volunteered.

Soon they were all at the field, and Duncan ran to warm up with his team while the others settled on the top bench to get a good view.

Duncan didn't disappoint as his family and Eli cheered like maniacs in the stands. Not that he ever needed an excuse to play well, but his desire to give his mom a great performance as a gift paid off. He broke the league record with five touchdowns and another record with three interceptions that day. His team won the game 45-7.

Everyone was in such a good mood afterward that the entire team decided to go to Highland Park Pizza for lunch. It was a chilly afternoon but nice enough for the kids to line up at one extended table outside and for the adults, along with Maddie and Eli, to line up along another row of tables pushed together.

It was just what the entire Trestin family needed as they tried to keep their minds off the bad news and Sheila's approaching chemotherapy that week. Nothing was a better distraction than a great game and tables full of laughing kids. Sheila was even able to stop worrying for a while and sit back to enjoy conversation with other parents, who she really didn't know very well, something that could sometimes be awkward.

Eli, of course, was a focus of attention for most of the kids who would run over to talk to him. To them, Eli was a local hero—someone they all aspired to be someday. This made Duncan feel special, too, since Eli was there because of him. Many of the dads also focused attention on Eli; they not only hoped their young boys would be as successful as he was on the football field, but they also loved reliving their own high school football days and sharing success stories with him.

Soon it was time to go, and the server brought out the bill and placed it in the middle of the table. Jake was sitting right there and grabbed it.

"I got this one," Jake offered.

Sheila shot Jake a quick look of concern. She knew this was something Jake liked doing, but she wasn't quite sure he should be doing it *now*. He didn't have a job, after all, and who knew what kind of medical bills they'd be racking up?

"Are you sure?" and "Let us help," came offers from other parents, but Jake refused.

"No, No. All good. This is my treat," Jake assured them.

Again, Sheila just looked quizzically at him.

"Don't worry, sweetheart. Let me do this one time. I'm sure we'll be fine," he whispered as he walked past her to pay inside. It was how he wanted to end this perfect day.

22

Sheila sat in the chair, waiting to start her first chemotherapy treatment. She almost wondered how she had even gotten there; the entire morning was such a blur.

She remembered staring at herself in the mirror that morning. She'd made a special effort to make her hair look extra nice. She knew it seemed silly, but she also knew she might not have hair much longer, so she wanted to appreciate it while she could. "Don't worry; it will grow back," she said aloud to herself.

Once her hair was done, looking the best it had in probably years, she looked into her eyes. Those beautiful Caribbean blue eyes that Jake had fallen in love with at first sight. Sure, she'd still have her eyes, but would they look all dark and sunken, surrounded by dark circles? She didn't know anyone personally who had gone through chemo, but she'd certainly seen enough cancer patients in the movies. "Is that how I'm going to look?" she was talking to herself again.

Sheila had been through so much the past week already, blood work, organ function tests, even a trip to the dentist, so she had already gotten used to pokes and prods and didn't even flinch when the needle slid into her vein. She sat back and was soon lost in her thoughts and memories. Tears filled her eyes, and she quickly wiped them away. She didn't feel bad physically, not yet anyway, but she kept thinking of Jake, Maddie, and Duncan. Would she be there to live out the next 50 years with them?

She thought back to her first 5 years of marriage. It was a wonderful period, as Jake and Sheila got used to one another's quirks and bad habits. They set up their first home together, and while they worked hard all week, they couldn't wait to spend every second of every weekend together.

They didn't even realize that anything had been missing until Maddie arrived. Then it instantly seemed like she'd been there forever, and neither Sheila nor Jake could ever imagine they had existed without her. And then Duncan. He added an energy that never slowed.

Every day with her family was an adventure, and until now, most of those adventures were good ones. Now she felt like she was speeding downhill on a roller coaster that had veered off track. Her heart ached at the thought that she might not be there to see her kids graduate from college, get married, and have kids of their own. Or would she even be there to see them graduate from high school?

She looked up and noticed that she was being "unhooked".

"Oh! Already? Believe it or not, that time flew by," Sheila managed a smile.

"Well, believe it or not, it might not seem like it right now, but you are one of the lucky ones. Some treatments take 5 times or more longer than yours."

"You are correct. I don't feel lucky," Sheila paused. "Actually, I guess I don't feel lucky on the one hand, but on the other hand, I do. I know things could be much worse."

"That's right. Please try to keep that in mind over the coming months." Margaret explained that she was the oncology nurse who would probably be giving Sheila most of her chemotherapy treatments. "We'll become quite close, you and I." She winked at Sheila and gave her hand a squeeze. "I'm going to walk you over to Dr. Beckham's office. Your husband will meet you there, and you can both talk to the doctor for a minute before you head home."

"Thanks, Margaret," Sheila said once arriving at the office. "I'll see you in a few days."

"Take care, Sheila. Please get plenty of rest and drink your fluids."

Jake gave Sheila a quick hug. "How did it go?"

"Not bad at all. I guess we'll see what comes next," she shrugged.

Dr. Beckham walked in and sat down. "One down and many more to go. How are you feeling, Sheila? Scared? Anxious? Confused? All the above?"

"Definitely all the above, but physically I feel fine."

"That's good. You probably won't feel bad after this first treatment. That, unfortunately, builds with each session. IF, it happens," she quickly added. "Remember, some people are lucky and don't feel sick with chemotherapy. And you have the medicine to help with that, too. Any questions before you head out of here?"

"No questions from me. Jake?" Sheila looked over at Jake.

"Not that I can think of right now. I'm sure we'll have many, but you've been very thorough, so I can't think of anything right now. And we have our cheat sheets to refer to if questions arise."

"Please call if you have any questions or concerns. You won't see me after every session, but I'll always get back to you if you call looking for me."

"Thanks, Dr. Beckham," Sheila and Jake replied in unison.

Once back in the car and on their way home, Sheila explained the process Margaret had taken her through. "It really wasn't bad, Jake, and I feel fine. As long as this remains the case, you don't have to bring me every time. It didn't take long, and I guess the side effects don't kick in right away after, so I should be fine driving."

"Well, we'll see how it goes."

Jake and Sheila were both silent for a while, both lost in their thoughts about all the uncertainty in their lives at the time.

"What times does your mom fly in tomorrow?" Jake asked.

"Sometime around 2:00, give or take. I can probably go get her," she paused. "Well, I guess we'll have to wait and see," her voice trailed.

Jake pulled into the driveway, but before pulling into the garage, Sheila looked at him, perplexed. "Why are the lights on? I'm pretty sure I turned them off when we left."

"You did? Well, that's weird. Maybe you thought you did but didn't."

They got out of the car and went inside. Sheila was surprised when she walked into the kitchen and there stood her mother.

"Mom!"

"Hi, honey. I couldn't wait another day to see you." Lee Sterling wrapped her arms around her daughter and both Mother and Daughter struggled to hold their composure.

23

Sheila and Lee stayed up late that night, catching up on everything going on in both of their lives. Sheila apologized to her mom for getting busy and so caught up in her own issues that she hadn't been calling her parents as much as she should or would like to do. They talked about everything, from Jake's job search, to her health issues, to her dad's refusal to retire, even though he was well past retirement age, and of course, to the excitement in her kids' lives.

Lee couldn't stay for more than a few days because she had her own doctors' appointments to get back to in Pennsylvania, and she couldn't leave Peter, Sheila's dad, home alone for too long, but she assured Sheila she would be back soon. They decided that, while she was there, they would do a bunch of cooking to load the freezer with meals that the Trestins could pop into the oven to easily reheat for dinner. Lee was a great cook, and she had passed those skills on to Sheila. Sheila was doing the same with Maddie and Duncan.

After the kids had left for school the next morning, they went grocery shopping and then got busy cooking. First, dozens of homemade meatballs that they cooked and froze in dinner-sized servings, then lasagna, which they separated into two meals after it was baked, then the family's favorite ground turkey and rice casserole, which they decided might be a little soggy after freezing and reheating but would still taste good.

As the ovens were baking these meals, they decided to make some soups. Jake made another run to the grocery store for them because they didn't have all the ingredients to now make chili and vegetable soup, but he was back in a flash. He grabbed a quick lunch for them all while he was out, so they sat together for lunch before starting on the soups. Sheila had powered through the morning and was now feeling a little tired and lacking in appetite, but she managed to eat half a sandwich and a few mixed greens.

Sheila didn't know how much more she'd be able to do in the kitchen that afternoon, but she got busy chopping vegetables while her mom worked on the chili. She was able to sit on a bar stool at the island so that she could be beside her mom while she chopped. Lee looked at her daughter and couldn't help but picture her as a teenager helping her cook on a Sunday afternoon. How had so much time passed so quickly? And how could her daughter be in a battle with cancer? She gave Sheila a loving half-smile.

"How are you doing, darling?"

"I'm doing OK, Mom. I'm just a little tired. I might lie down for a while after we are done with this soup."

"Why don't you just finish what you are doing, and I'll finish the soup. You've done the tedious chore of veggie chopping. I can easily throw everything into the pot with the meat. Then you can rest a little before the kids come home."

"OK, thanks, Mom," Sheila sighed, grateful that her mom had made the suggestion. She finished the two carrots that lay on her cutting board and headed upstairs to rest for a bit.

Sheila fell asleep immediately upon climbing into the bed and couldn't believe her eyes the next time she opened them. It was 5:30, and she had slept for 3 hours. She felt as though she could go back to sleep and stay there until morning, but she didn't want to do that. She stretched, rubbed her eyes, and went downstairs to see what she was missing.

She laughed when she walked into the kitchen and both Maddie and Duncan were there with Lee.

"Still cooking, Mom?" Sheila asked.

"Mom!" Both Maddie and Duncan exclaimed and ran over to greet their mom.

"Grammy is baking cookies with us," Duncan explained.

"Yes, I had just finished cleaning up from our day of cooking when the kids got home. So we decided to mess up the kitchen again," Lee laughed.

"I'm making sugar cookies, and Duncan is making chocolate chip," Maddie informed her mom. "And I told Duncan he has to help with the baking and the cleaning up after. He can't just run off after he's done mixing them up, and then come back to eat them after they come out of the oven. Not fair!" Maddie loved teasing her brother.

"You know what? I'm feeling kind of hungry. I think I'll have some of both—sugar *and* chocolate chip," Sheila requested. "And milk."

"OK, Mom, but not too many. You need to watch your sugar intake," Duncan scolded his mother.

"Hey! Come on! You can't make cookies, then tell me I can't have any," Sheila implored. "But you are right. And it's almost dinnertime, so none of us should be eating too many cookies."

"OK, Mom," Maddie agreed as she pulled the milk out of the fridge and poured her mom a glass.

"Where's your dad?" Sheila asked her children.

"Oh. He ran out to get dinner. You were asleep, and we were baking, so he didn't want anyone to worry about it," Maddie explained.

"Good thing we loaded the freezer, Mom," Sheila looked at Lee with a concerned expression. "We'd go broke with all of this ordering dinner."

"We ordered you salmon, couscous, and sauteed spinach," Duncan informed her.

"Sounds both delicious and healthy. Thank you." Sheila couldn't help but worry about spending the extra money on expensive meals for dinner. She decided she should talk about it with Jake later.

Just about then, Jake walked in. "Are you guys eating cookies while I'm out picking up dinner?"

"Hi, sweetheart. I just couldn't help myself," Sheila laughed.

"How was your nap? Are you feeling better?" Jake inquired with a quick hug.

"I didn't feel bad. I was just tired, and yes, I feel better. Just being here with you all—and eating cookies—makes me feel better."

"And salmon for dessert!" Jake laughed. They all laughed.

"Here, Jake." Lee handed $150 to him. "Dinner is on me."

"Lee, it's fine. You don't have to do that. You flew here. The least I could do is feed you for a few days."

"Will you please just let me treat my family to a nice dinner at home? I rarely get to do it."

Jake begrudgingly reached over and accepted the cash.

24

Duncan woke up on Saturday morning, determined to have a repeat of the previous Saturday. He was disappointed when he looked outside and saw that it had rained overnight and was gray and very windy. "That's OK," he told himself. At least it had stopped raining, and the game shouldn't be canceled.

He went to begin his new game-day morning ritual. First a shower, then downstairs for his usual breakfast. When he got to the kitchen, he saw his breakfast sandwich and a bowl of fresh fruit sitting at his spot, but he didn't see his mom.

"Hi, Grammy. Where's Mom?" was his greeting.

"Good morning, Duncan. Mom's a little tired this morning, and I don't think it would be good for her to be outside in the weather today, anyway."

"Oh." Duncan looked down, disappointed.

"But she told me exactly how to make your breakfast, so I hope it's OK."

"I'm sure it is. Thanks."

Soon Jake joined Duncan at the table. "I'm sorry, Mom can't go today, Dunc, but Grammy is going with us."

"You are?" Duncan's spirits lifted.

"Of course, I am! Do you think I'd come all this way and not see my favorite grandson play football?" Lee winked at Duncan.

"Haha, Grammy. I'm your only grandson." Duncan scrunched up his face and rolled his eyes, trying to add a little humor to his grandmother's corny joke.

Before leaving, Duncan went in to see Sheila. She'd had her second chemo treatment a couple of days before, and while she didn't feel too awful, she was very tired.

"Goodbye, Mom. Get some rest, and I'll tell you all about the game when I get home." Duncan kissed her on the forehead.

"Have a great game, buddy. I'm sorry I can't be there in person, but you know I'll be there in spirit. Maybe next week, OK?"

"Sure."

Duncan tried to shake off his sadness and joined Jake, Lee, and Maddie, who were heading to the car.

"Oh! Hold on. I almost forgot my water bottle."

Duncan made a mental note to start trying harder to remember things now that his mom wouldn't always be available to remind him.

"Isn't Eli coming today, either?" Duncan asked Maddie disappointedly, as he climbed into the car.

"He's coming, but he's driving separately because of the weather. That way, he can drive me home if it gets too nasty. And Grammy, too," Maddie explained and grabbed Lee's hand, who had sat in the back seat beside Maddie so that Duncan could ride up front.

Eli was already at the field when they got there. "I'm not afraid of a little drizzle," he laughed and told Duncan.

He was still riding high after the big win the night before. The Titans were undefeated so far this season.

The game had a shaky start, as the grass was wet and slippery. Some of the boys didn't have good cleats and they had a hard time getting any traction. Duncan was wearing good cleats so he wasn't worried about that. However, what he wasn't counting on was another player, his own teammate, slipping and sliding into Duncan. His knee felt a little sore after he stood up following the collision, but he was able to walk it off and keep playing.

"Flag football can still be very rough," Eli was explaining to Lee. "The kids play very hard, and they still do a lot of falling, colliding, and even flipping sometimes."

"Flipping?" Lee was alarmed at the sound of that. "And they don't even wear helmets!"

Just about then, Duncan leaped in the end zone for his second touchdown of the game. As he landed, he collapsed to the ground in pain. He lay in the endzone holding his knee.

The coaches ran out to check on him, and it was all Jake, Maddie, and Lee could do to keep from running out to him, too. The coaches knelt on the field with Duncan, talking with him and checking his knee. When they got up to help him to the sidelines, they looked up in the stands and waved for Jake to come down. All four of them jumped up and went to the sidelines.

"It's his knee," Coach told them. "I guess he strained it during the collision earlier, and he says he landed on it wrong after his catch."

"It really hurts, Dad." Duncan was trying very hard not to cry, but his eyes were a little teary from the pain and from the disappointment.

"I think you should probably take him to the ER to get him checked out," Coach continued.

"OK. Thanks, Coach. We'll head over there now. Sorry you have to finish the game without him," he said, shaking the coaches' hands. "And I'm sorry, Dunc. Let's go get you checked out."

"Hang in there, Duncan. You're tough, and you'll be OK," Eli encouraged him. "There's no need for Maddie and your grandma to go sit at the hospital, so I'll give them a ride home."

"Thanks, Eli. We really appreciate that," Jake said and patted him on the shoulder.

"Bye, Dunc-y. I love you." Maddie was very sad for her brother.

"So do I," Lee chimed in. "I'm glad I got to see some great play before you went down. You were amazing!"

"Thanks, Grammy," Duncan winced.

It was 5 hours later when Jake and Duncan finally came into the house. Duncan was using crutches.

"We were lucky that there was a top orthopedist on call today," Jake explained, "so we were able to have all x-rays and MRIs done today."

"I don't know whether I'd use the word 'lucky', Dad," Duncan grumbled.

"Well, you have a good point there, but I mean, we don't have to go back for another appointment right away."

"What did he say?" Sheila had been extremely anxious since the others had arrived home.

"The good news is that he doesn't need surgery," Jake explained, putting his arm around Duncan.

"The bad news is that I can't play any more football this season. And I probably can't play basketball either." And with that, Duncan broke down in tears. Then he quickly looked at his mom and stopped crying. "But I'm OK," he told her.

"They want him to start some physical therapy this week," Jake continued.

"That's quick. He doesn't have to recover any first?" Sheila asked.

"He needs to do ice on and ice off every 20 minutes for the next 24 hours, but they want him to start strengthening it right away," Jake answered.

"I'm so sorry, kiddo." Sheila hugged her son tight. "Let's get your strength up and get some dinner in you. I sent Eli and Maddie to the store when they got home, and I made you tacos."

"Thanks, Mom," Duncan mustered a smile. "I'll try to eat, but I don't have much of an appetite."

25

Jake lay awake in bed for most of the night, Sunday night into Monday. He couldn't believe the awful state his family seemed to be in right now. First and foremost, was Sheila's health. He couldn't stand to think of her not beating her cancer, so he wouldn't do that, but even just knowing what she was going through with her treatments was devastating to him. And now Duncan was hurt, too.

He knew Duncan was young and resilient and would bounce back, but he was so disappointed for him. Duncan had been having a great football season, and he was so excited for his basketball season. Between those two sports, he barely spoke of anything else. He had been a trooper and was very diligent about icing his knee and even knocking out his homework during the day on Sunday, but Jake knew Duncan was suffering inside.

Jake took comfort in the fact that Maddie was in such a good place, despite being upset for her mom and brother. He hoped that would continue. He knew how fragile young romance could be.

But it wasn't only the health issues of his wife and son that bothered him. He made calls every day and followed every lead he could find, but he'd had no luck finding a new job. He had received a nice severance package when he lost his job, but his health insurance wouldn't last forever, and his family was really racking up the medical bills. He had saved money for many years, but he didn't want to spend it all now on living expenses and medical bills. It wouldn't last nearly long enough at this rate, and he didn't want his family to end up broke.

He lay awake, contemplating many things. Should he borrow money from his parents? No, that would be the last alternative. He didn't want to dig into his parents' retirement savings, not without knowing how quickly he'd be able to pay them back. Should he take a lower-level job just to have some money coming in?

He knew he'd have trouble finding a job that way, too, because employers are hesitant to hire someone who is overqualified, knowing that person has no intention of staying in the job. Sheila had been planning to do some freelance work, but there's no way he wanted her to take that on right now.

Once he finally fell into a light sleep, he still tossed and turned, half dreaming and half lying awake and thinking. He wasn't sure he'd gotten even 2 hours of sleep when he climbed out of bed and turned off the alarm before it even made a sound because he didn't want it to wake up Sheila. He was already awake, so he figured he might as well go eat breakfast with the kids and, more importantly, see how Duncan was doing.

He had decided to opt out of the carpool that morning and drive the kids to school himself. He wanted to go into the school office to talk about Duncan's situation and special needs with school administrators. Duncan would need help with his books, and he'd also need an extra chair on which to put his leg. He was supposed to keep it elevated for a few more days.

Jake knocked lightly on Duncan's door and slowly pushed it open. Duncan was sitting on the edge of the bed and had already changed out of his pajamas and into his clothes.

"It's supposed to be pretty chilly today, Duncan," Jake pointed out, looking at Duncan's choice to wear shorts.

"I know, Dad, but with the bulkiness of the brace on my knee, it's just easier to wear shorts. My joggers or sweats wouldn't even stretch out enough. I'll just wear a hoodie. I'll be fine."

"OK. Well, let's get you down to breakfast. How can I help you?"

"Just grab my backpack, please. I'll give you one of my crutches when we get to the steps. I'll use the other one to help myself down the steps."

Maddie was already in the kitchen with Lee when Jake and Duncan made their way downstairs.

Maddie still had a soft spot in her heart for Duncan and his bum knee, so she had gotten up early to make him scrambled eggs and bacon. Lee had also made some fresh biscuits that she was pulling out of the oven. "You can either eat these on the side or make a sandwich with your eggs and bacon. I know you love breakfast sandwiches."

"Thanks, Grammy. And thanks, Mad." Duncan mustered a smile for his grandmother and sister. He didn't really feel like eating, but he didn't want to make them feel bad after they had made an extra effort to make him a special breakfast.

Plus, as his father had already reminded him, he needed something in his stomach so that he could take some of the prescription ibuprofen the hospital had sent home with him. Surprising the rest of his family, as well as himself, he finished every bite on his plate. The food tasted very good, and he was hungrier than he thought since he hadn't been eating much since his injury, even though they had leftover taco ingredients from Friday night.

Jake had soon delivered Maddie and Duncan to school, gone into the school office to talk about Duncan's special needs, and was on his way home again when he drove past something he had never really noticed before.

About half a mile from the school was a temporary corporate apartment complex. While he hadn't paid attention to it in the past, he did recognize the name, Your Home Apartments, as the place where new employees would stay when they first moved into town and hadn't yet found a permanent residence. He knew they were furnished apartments and wondered how much they cost per month.

He hurried into the house and grabbed his laptop as soon as he got home. He was reading about the apartments at the kitchen table when Sheila walked in.

"Good morning, Jake," Sheila smiled at her husband.

"Good morning, sweetheart. Sit down. What can I get you?"

"Just a little juice for now, please. I might have some oatmeal in a bit, but just juice for now. Thanks."

"Here you go." Jake set down a glass of cranberry juice in front of her. "I barely slept at all last night."

"I know. You tossed and turned all night long," Sheila acknowledged.

"I'm so sorry. Did I keep you awake?"

"No, you didn't bother me. I just noticed that every time I woke up, you were awake, too. Is everything OK? Are you worried about Duncan?"

"Ha! That's a bit of an understatement. I'm worried about Duncan; I'm worried about you; I'm worried about me and my lack of an income."

"We'll be OK, Jake. Somehow, we'll figure it all out," Sheila reassured him.

"Well, I was worried about it all night, not to mention every second of every day." Jake paused and looked down at his hands on the table for a few seconds, wondering how to bring up his idea to Sheila and whether it was the right time.

He continued, "It seems like one thing after another keeps coming at us. It's like a hurricane of bad news that is constantly swirling around in my head." He paused and took a deep breath, realizing he might as well just say it.

"But when I was driving home from school this morning, I drove past something that caught my eye."

"Yeah?" Sheila inquired.

"You know those temporary apartments on Smith Avenue, Your Home Apartments? I've been doing some research, and we can get a 2-bedroom apartment, maybe even a 3-bedroom, for a pretty decent price. And they are even furnished."

"I don't understand, Jake. We have a home. What exactly are you suggesting? That we sell the house?" Sheila started to get a little upset and worried.

"No, no. Don't worry. I'm just brainstorming, but as you know, our house payment is a very big expense every month. But people pay even more for rent. I need to think about how we would do this, but we could rent out the house for 6 months or a year or so, or we could rent it out as a vacation home on one of those websites, or we could even rent it out as temporary corporate housing. We would make enough to pay the mortgage and the rent for an apartment and still have a little left to help with daily living expenses."

Sheila looked at him, surprised. "Wow. It sounds like you've already put a lot of thought into this."

"Not really. It was just an idea that came to me when I drove past the apartments this morning. And Sheila—" Jake paused. "I think it would be easier for *all* of us while you are going through chemo to have a smaller place to take care of and clean. The kids and I would be able to keep an apartment clean without your thinking you need to clean up after us. Despite how many times we tell you not to do it, you can't help yourself."

"I agree with that," Lee chimed in as she entered the kitchen. She had caught the end of the conversation as she paused in the other room before entering.

"OK. Let's look into it a little more," Sheila conceded. "I know we aren't keeping secrets, but let's not mention it to the kids until we've looked into it a little more and know it's a possibility."

26

Maddie burst through the front door after getting dropped off after school. She almost forgot that her brother was hobbling up the sidewalk behind her. "Oh shoot," she mumbled to herself as she ran back to help Duncan and hold the door open for him.

"Mom?" she called softly, hoping her mother wasn't asleep.

"I'm in the family room, Maddie. How did your day go, Duncan?" Sheila was anxious to hear how Duncan felt.

"It was fine, Mom. Don't worry about me," Duncan reassured her.

"Mom," Maddie jumped in, "with everything going on, we forgot to talk about the Homecoming dance. I was really hoping for a new dress; I don't think I have anything appropriate to wear."

"Oh my gosh, Maddie. We haven't talked about this at all. When is the dance? I'm sure we can go shopping to find a little something new."

"It's this weekend. The Homecoming game is Friday night, and the dance is Saturday night. Eli asked me a while ago, but we've had so much going on that I just didn't even mention it."

"Maddie, that's so exciting. I can't believe you didn't share this with me. Please don't ever think that I have too much going on to share your life with you."

"Sorry," Maddie looked down. She had felt a little guilty about being so excited about something when her mom was going through something so terrible.

"Let's plan to go tomorrow. Grammy can help us. She'll love it, too. And I'll make sure I take a little nap after lunch tomorrow so that I can save up some energy for the mall." Sheila made a mental note to look later at the mall directory. They might have to shop in some stores where they usually would not shop. And she really hoped for some sales!

The excitement about Homecoming and shopping for a new dress helped carry both Maddie and Sheila through the next 24 hours. Maddie spent hours on the phone with Gabby, talking about what kind of dress she wanted and looking at websites full of dresses to get ideas. She also checked with Eli to see what he would be wearing.

He sent her a picture of his blue suit with two different options of shirts and ties. Maddie decided she would find a dress to pull out the same color in one of his ties. She still couldn't believe she was dating Eli Schwartz and would be walking into the dance with him!

When Maddie, Sheila, and Lee got to the mall, they decided to start at one end and work their way to the other end. They thought this method would be the easiest for Sheila, rather than hitting all their usual spots first and having to walk back and forth. Plus, Sheila secretly hoped they would find something Maddie loved before making it to the more expensive stores at the other end of the mall.

She had strategically made sure she parked at this end of the mall.

The Town Center was a very big mall, and they went into store after store after store. Maddie wasn't one to waste much time if she didn't see what she wanted. She wasn't having any luck and was getting increasingly frustrated. Either she didn't like any of the dresses in a shop, or they didn't have a dress she liked in her size, or she liked a dress and they had her size, but it was the wrong color and wouldn't match either of Eli's ties.

"How about if Eli just gets a new tie to match your dress?" Lee laughed, trying to keep the mood light.

"I don't want him to have to worry about that, Grammy. He's too busy this week with practice and school," Maddie whined.

"And Eli probably couldn't care less if his tie and Maddie's dress match," Sheila chuckled.

Maddie tried hard not to huff and walk away, but she didn't quite succeed. In the meantime, Sheila grew increasingly worried as they quickly approached the more upscale end of the mall. She didn't realize it, but Maddie also had the same worry, which was another reason she was getting increasingly irritated.

The next store they went into gave both mom and daughter a little hope. It was actually an outlet for one of their favorite upscale department stores, and luck was on their side; they not only had a fall sale but also a huge selection from which to pick! Maddie quickly pulled seven dresses off the clearance rack to try on and practically ran to the fitting room.

She tried on five of the dresses before she even came out to show Sheila and Lee, but when she finally came out, the jaws of both Mom and Grandmother dropped. Sheila got a tear in her eye. "That's the one, Maddie," Sheila assured her.

It was a jade-green fitted dress that stopped just above her knees. The back was open in a V and was cut pretty low but not low enough to upset her father.

"You'll need some pasties, but I saw those on display over by the cash register. And I have the perfect necklace that you can borrow," Sheila offered.

"And I can wear my silver shoes. I don't need to get new ones," Maddie grinned.

Lee shook her head. "You are absolutely stunning in that dress, Maddie."

"Thanks, Grammy. I'm not so sure I'm stunning now, but I will be on Saturday night," Maddie laughed and posed. Sheila and Lee laughed and quickly agreed.

After Maddie changed back into her clothes, and as they walked over to get in line, something else on the wall rack caught Maddie's eye. She grabbed the pasties by the line to the register, then told her mom to go out and have a seat on the bench outside the store. "Grammy and I will buy the dress, then come out to meet you. You don't need to stand in this long line with us."

<h1 style="text-align:center">27</h1>

The entire Trestin family was excited on Friday morning before the big Homecoming game that evening. Jake and Sheila were happy to see that Duncan's spirits were lifted a little. He had barely shown a smile since his knee injury. He'd have to hobble to the game on crutches, but at least he was going.

Everyone had something to do to pass the day. Maddie and Duncan were headed to school, of course; Jake had a meeting with a former colleague; and Lee was headed to the grocery store. Sheila had her own little 'surprise' for the family and was anxious to have the house to herself. After everyone had given their respective hugs and kisses goodbye, Sheila sat and finished her cup of mint tea, then just sat for about 20 minutes almost in a meditative state.

"Welp, I might as well get this over with," she told herself as she finally snapped herself out of it.

Sheila went upstairs to the master bathroom and pulled out the chair at her vanity "make-up" desk. She pulled out the bottom drawer and removed an electric razor that she had secretly ordered online. Her hands were shaking as she opened the box and wondered what she would look like with a bald head.

She sat there looking at and playing with her hair for a few more minutes. Her family hadn't said anything, but there was no way they hadn't noticed her hair thinning. And she had already started wearing hats and scarves, so they were used to that. They certainly couldn't be too surprised when they came home and found her hair was all gone. She hoped they wouldn't be upset that she hadn't warned them. For some reason, Sheila couldn't find the mental strength to talk about it and tell them. She just needed to do it.

Sheila reached back into the drawer and pulled out the scissors that she had hidden with the razor. "Here it goes," she said out loud to her reflection in the mirror. She cut big chunks of her hair and laid it on the vanity in front of her. Then she took the razor and made a path straight through the center of her head.

For some reason, she couldn't resist the urge to laugh. She supposed it was a coping mechanism. *I've had enough crying,* she thought. Besides, she did look pretty funny with chopped-up clumps of hair and a bald path through the middle of her head. She thought for a second about taking a picture but quickly decided against it.

Once she had finished shaving her head, she rubbed her hands all over her bald head. She sighed and felt that she was actually pretty lucky. She had a pretty smooth and round head—no major dents or blemishes. She then took a shower to wash away all the little pieces of hair. When she got out of the shower, she wondered whether to use face moisturizer on her head or just regular lotion. Then she laughed at herself again. So many questions one doesn't think about until the moment.

Lee was the first to come home and find Sheila still upstairs getting dressed. "Oh, honey," she exclaimed as soon as she saw Sheila. "You look beautiful!" She quickly recovered. "I didn't think it was possible, but your eyes stand out even more without the distraction of your hair." They both laughed at that comment until they had tears streaming down their faces and then mused about their instinct to laugh in this situation.

Lee then asked for Sheila's permission to help her put on some make-up. She knew Sheila didn't need her help, but it seemed like the motherly thing to do, and she just wanted to do something for her daughter.

As they were finishing up, they heard Jake come in downstairs. "Uh oh." Shelia looked at her mom.

"It will be fine, Sheila. Jake loves you, hair or no hair. And you still look gorgeous!" Lee assured her.

"Sheila?" Jake called out as he entered the room and looked for his wife. He didn't seem at all phased by what he saw and walked over and embraced Sheila. He then kissed her on the top of her bald head. He pulled back and gave her a warm smile. "Your head might get a little chilly at the game tonight," he mentioned.

"Don't worry," Sheila smiled back at him. "I already thought of that. I grabbed Duncan's black and red ski cap from his room and washed it. Luckily, it's school colors; I'll blend right in."

The conversations with Maddie and Duncan were similar when they arrived home from school, but everyone was too excited for the evening to dwell on anything sad. It seemed to be an unspoken agreement—they would have a fun evening, despite anything else going on in their lives.

Maddie had plans to leave early to grab pizza with some of her friends before the game. Claire had agreed to drive the group of girls to dinner and the game, so she and Gabby ran in quickly to say hello.

Claire gave Sheila a big squeeze. "Shall we meet up by the concession stand at 7:00? Then we can all find a seat together."

Jake and Sheila agreed that was a good plan but decided they'd get there a little early to get Duncan settled in the stands with his friends.

"We better get going then, too," Jake suggested. "Let's grab a bite to eat at the diner. There's no reason to make a mess that we'll have to come home to after the game."

"Great idea," Lee agreed. "Before we go, let's grab a couple of blankets and scarves. And don't forget that hat, Sheila. Where is it? I'll get it."

Sheila was already feeling a little tired when they got to the football stadium, but she refused to let it dampen her spirits or her fun. She bundled up, cuddled between her mom and husband, and enjoyed her ties to the star player.

Maddie, meanwhile, sat with her friends in the top row of the stands. She wanted to have a wide view of the entire field. She didn't want to miss one play of the game, well, at least not the offensive drives.

Duncan, who normally would have spent much of the game walking around and goofing off with his friends, was happy to actually sit and watch the entire game. He always wanted to watch every play of every game, but his friends usually convinced him to cruise the crowd. He was glad he had the excuse to stay put in his seat at this game. His friends also enjoyed staying in the stands to watch.

Eli again led the Titans to a victory against their rival school, 24-7. As soon as the game was over, Maddie found her parents and asked whether Eli could drive her home. "Don't worry. I'm coming right home. The team is meeting for post-game pizza, but Eli texted that he wants to drop me off on the way. Is that OK? Please."

"That's fine, sweetheart," Sheila told her. "We'll see you at home."

"Oh! Also," Maddie added. "Is it OK if Gabby spends the night tomorrow after the dance? We'll probably stay up all night talking," she laughed.

"Of course," Jake answered. "Since when isn't it OK to have Gabby spend the night?"

28

Sheila was still completely exhausted when Jake crawled out of bed the next morning. She had gotten pretty chilly at the game the night before, and it had taken her a while to warm up after climbing into bed. Once she fell asleep, she hardly moved the entire night.

Jake was awake enough overnight to keep track of his wife's entire night. He could also tell Sheila needed more sleep when she could barely manage a mumble to him when he climbed out of bed. He was surprised to see Maddie when she walked into the kitchen shortly after he had gone in to get some coffee.

"You're up much earlier than I expected," Jake teased her. "Don't you have about 4 more hours to sleep? It is Saturday morning, after all."

"I know," Maddie whined. "I wanted to sleep longer so that I won't get tired tonight, but I'm just too excited. My mind kept racing about everything I need to do. I need to do some homework, but I want to save a lot of time to get ready so that I'm not rushed," she paused. "Do you think Mom will be up to helping me get ready? I thought it would be something special we could do together."

"I think there is nothing she would rather do. I know she's almost as excited for tonight as you are. This is a big deal for her—her daughter's first high school dance." Jake hoped he wasn't over-promising. He knew Sheila was exhausted. She'd had a big day on Friday and might need a little recovery time. "We'll just let her sleep as late as possible."

"Great idea," Maddie agreed as she poured herself coffee. "I better have a couple of cups of coffee today," she added as she headed back to her room to knock out the homework.

"Good morning, Lee. Thanks for making coffee," Jake said as Lee walked in.

"No problem. I was up. Do you want something to eat?" Lee offered.

"No, I'm not hungry. Thanks for offering, but don't worry; I can make it myself when I want something," Jake defended. "Can we talk a minute?"

"Of course. What's on your mind?"

Jake and Sheila had decided to move ahead with the plan to rent out their house for a currently undetermined amount of time, but they hadn't yet explained their plan to Lee. She sat and listened as Jake detailed the plan.

"We are stretching our budget as much as possible to get a 3-bedroom, so as long as you are with us—and you are welcome to stay as long as you want—I'm afraid you'll either have to sleep with Maddie in a double bed or sleep on the sofa. I'm sorry, Lee. We just think this is the smartest thing to do right now."

"Jake, you never need to apologize to me for doing what's best for your family. I don't care where I sleep." Lee looked down at her hands. "But honestly, I think I need to head home for a while, anyway. I'm being a little missed at home and have some of my own appointments on my schedule." Lee's voice cracked, and her eyes teared up a little. "I hope that's OK with you and Sheila. I hate to leave her like this."

"Lee, you've done so much for us already, and we've loved having you here. But you have your own life to get back to—"

"Sheila is my life," Lee interrupted. "Nothing is more important to me."

"I know that, and you are always welcome to come back whenever and as soon as you like." Jake forced a laugh. "You'll just have to sleep on a sofa."

Lee smiled and put her hand on Jake's. "I won't mind that at all," she assured him. "And I'll probably be back sooner than you want. I just need to take care of a few things at home, including your father-in-law," she laughed.

"Good morning. You two look cozy. What am I missing?" Sheila asked as she wandered in.

"Oh, not much," Jake answered as he jumped up to pull out a chair for her.

"Let me make you some mint tea," Lee offered, grabbing a cup from the dishwasher.

"I wish I hadn't given up caffeine. I sure could use some this morning," Sheila groaned.

"We should start making decaf coffee for you. I don't know why we didn't think of that sooner. Even without the caffeine, you'd feel like you aren't missing as much. I'll give up the caffeine with you," Jake offered.

"I thought I heard music coming from Maddie's room. Is she up already?" Sheila inquired.

"She is. She's knocking out some homework, then plans to spend the rest of the day preparing for her big night," Jake explained. "And she's hoping for some special mother/daughter time in the process."

Sheila's body posture changed with that suggestion. "She is? Well, all it takes is a little cancer to get my daughter to spend more time with me," she chuckled.

Sheila drank her tea, ate a small bowl of oatmeal with berries and honey, and went back upstairs to take a shower. She couldn't have her caffeine, so she thought a little nourishment and a hot shower could help wake her up. She wasn't going to let anything get in the way of her special time with Maddie.

Maddie was growing up so quickly, and Sheila was realizing how quickly the years flew by. She knew her time with her kids was limited. It seemed like Maddie had just been a little girl heading off to preschool with her mom's kiss in her hand. Now she was headed off to her first high school dance. With a boyfriend! Before she knew it, she'd be heading off to college.

Sheila felt much better once she had showered and gotten dressed. She went to Maddie's room and knocked softly on the door. "Hey, kiddo," she whispered as she pushed open the door.

"Hi, Mom. I'm just finishing up the first draft of my English paper. Want to have lunch with me, then you can help me get ready? Well, I have to shower first, then you can help me."

"Of course, I want to help you! I'm glad you want me to help you. Is there anything in particular you want me to do?"

"Actually, yes. I want you to help me with my hair. I thought we could curl it a little and then figure out some kind of half up/half down hairdo."

"Sounds great. I have some hair accessories we can use. I'll grab some things while you are taking your shower." She looked at Maddie with a small grin. "I sure don't have any use for them."

"Mom," Maddie assured her. "You'll be using them again soon enough."

"Let's go get lunch. What sounds good to you?"

"Let's go look. I'm not sure what I want. I'm so excited about tonight that my stomach has butterflies—and they aren't saving much room for food."

Sheila laughed. "Go on down. I haven't seen Duncan today, so I want to pop into his room."

"Hey, buddy," Sheila greeted Duncan as she pushed open his cracked door. Duncan was still in bed but was wide awake.

"Hi, Mom." He just stared at the ceiling.

"Maddie and I are going to have some lunch. Will you join us?"

"I guess," Duncan answered with little expression.

"You doing OK?"

"Yep."

"OK, well, if you want to talk about anything, you know Dad and I are here."

"Yep." Duncan climbed out of bed. "What's for lunch? I'm starving."

"I'm sure you are. It's 1:30, and you haven't eaten. Let's go find something."

Jake and Lee both joined the others in the kitchen, where they decided on chicken Caesar salads for lunch. Lee cut up leftover chicken breasts from earlier in the week while Maddie and Duncan put together the salads.

As they ate, Maddie explained the plans for the evening. Eli would arrive at 5:30 so that they would have time to take some pictures before making their 6:00 dinner reservation. Jorge and Gabby, and Mike and his date, Julie, would also arrive in a separate car. They had a reservation for the six of them, and they thought it would be fun to get pictures together ahead of time, especially since Maddie and Gabby were best friends, as were Eli and Mike.

As soon as they were done eating, Maddie went up to take her shower. Sheila asked Lee to come help her find some appropriate hair accessories. She was pretty sure she had some clips in a box that would either match or at least accompany Maddie's dress or her silver shoes. They sat on the bed and pulled out several things they thought would work.

Maddie soon walked in, freshly showered and wearing her robe. Lee took that as her cue to leave to allow mother and daughter some alone time.

Maddie sat in her mother's chair at the vanity, and Sheila pulled out the hair dryer, another thing she wouldn't use on herself for a while.

Sheila was excited to be helping Maddie with her hair. It was something she used to do every day when Maddie was younger, but Maddie hadn't needed the help since she decided to stop the braids, pigtails, and ponytails every day.

Her hair was so pretty that Sheila was happy when Maddie decided to start wearing it down, but she missed the morning ritual of helping her with it.

Sheila dried Maddie's hair and then added some big curls with the curling iron. Together they experimented with different clips, pins, and bands and decided on long and flowy in the back and loosely pulled up on the sides. As Maddie started her make-up, Sheila went into her bedroom to pick out something nicer to wear.

"Wait, Mom!" Maddie called after her. "Sit down a minute. I have something for you."

"You do? Oh, OK. This is exciting."

Maddie ran to her room and was back in about 10 seconds. She handed Sheila a gift bag that she had dug out of the box full of gift wrap supplies in the linen closet in the hallway.

"Maddie, what's this for?" Sheila inquired as she pulled out a beautiful jade scarf with silver highlights and border.

"I want to get some pictures with you tonight, and I thought this scarf would match my dress perfectly," Maddie's voice shook a little.

"Oh, Maddie. It's gorgeous. Where did you find this?"

"Grammy helped me get it. I saw it when I got my dress. Remember when I sent you out to sit in the mall while we paid for the dress?"

"Well, aren't you sneaky!" Sheila smiled at her daughter. "I would love to take some pictures with you."

"Thanks, Mom."

"Thank you! In fact, why don't we make Dad and Duncan put on something nice, too, and we can have Grammy take some pictures of the four of us together before everyone gets here? And we can have Dad take some of us with Grammy.”

“Sounds like a plan,” Maddie agreed.

“Now help me find something to wear that will look nice with this beautiful scarf. And then you can help me figure out how to wrap it around my head.”

29

Pictures were taken, hugs were given, and soon Maddie and Eli were at dinner with their friends. They had decided on a seafood restaurant that was between Maddie's house and the school. They thought that would be the easiest place to eat without having to add much drive time to their evening. Plus, Maddie and Eli both loved salmon, so they selfishly chose a restaurant where they could get good salmon.

They were all having such a good time reliving the football game the night before and complaining about school that they didn't realize how late it was getting. Eli, Mike, Jorge, and Julie, all juniors, had also been talking about SAT and ACT prep and thinking ahead to which colleges they might apply. These subjects were still very foreign to Maddie and Gabby, and they were a little intimidated by the older kids. They had barely started high school, and the others were already talking about college.

"Come on, guys. Maddie and Gabby don't care about test prep yet. Let's talk about something of more interest to them," Julie tried to change the subject.

"Actually, we should pay and get going. Look what time it is," Jorge interjected.

None of them yet had a credit card, so they each pulled out their phones to do the math, and then their wallets to count out what they owed. The boys insisted on paying for dinner and told the girls they could pay for the after-dance desserts. They had all decided to extend the evening a little longer by heading to the diner for dessert after the dance.

When they walked into the gym that the student government had decorated for the dance, Maddie quickly realized there wouldn't be much talking. The music boomed so loudly that no one could hear each other talk. They quickly hit the photo booth and then went straight to the dance floor. It would be more an evening of exercising the body than one of exercising the mouth and ears.

They danced song after song after song, then decided they needed a quick drink. As they grabbed some punch and went to a table to sit for a minute, Eli excused himself to the bathroom. He came back a couple of minutes later and sat down to finish his punch. Just a minute later, a mischievous smile creeped across his face as Maddie's head jerked up to look at him. Then she started laughing as Eli grabbed her hand and pulled her back onto the dance floor. The others joined them but didn't quite understand what was so funny.

Maddie lay her head on Eli's chest as they listened and swayed to Air Supply's *All Out of Love.* She sang along in her head and didn't want the song to end. She was so happy and felt as though she could stay just like that forever. "Could life be any better?" she wondered. "Well, I guess so," she quickly reminded herself, "if Mom didn't have cancer and Dad had a job!" But she quickly put those thoughts out of her head. Nothing could be better than being there in Eli's arms.

The dance was soon over, and the six of them drove to the diner. They'd had big dinners before the dance, but they were all ready for a snack after all of that dancing. They decided on some appetizers before their desserts, so they ordered some mozzarella sticks and chicken tenders for the table, and then each chose his or her own dessert. Maddie decided on a slice of banana cream pie, and Eli ordered a crème Brulé.

"That looks really good," Eli smiled at Maddie. "Bite for bite?" he asked.

"OK," Maddie laughed back at him. "I might steal more than one bite. I almost ordered that myself."

They proceeded to take turns taking a bite of each dessert one after the other, giggling and teasing each other the entire time.

"You two are crazy," Mike rolled his eyes at them.

"No, they aren't," Julie defended them, punching Mike in the arm. "They are cute."

"They're in loooo-ooove," Jorge teased.

Gabby quickly decided she better jump in and rescue her best friend. She felt an awkward moment approaching with the mention of the 'L word'.

"What's everyone doing tomorrow?" Gabby quickly threw out.

"Sleeping!" Eli answered.

"And then probably some more homework." Maddie rolled her eyes.

"And on that note, we better get going," Julie prompted. "I don't know about you guys, but I still have a curfew tonight."

The girls paid, and they all walked to their cars. Instead of getting in the car with Mike and Julie, Jorge and Gabby got into the car with Eli and Maddie. Maddie was glad Gabby was spending the night because they had a lot to talk about and break down, but she was also sorry she would no longer be in the car alone with Eli. She hadn't really had any alone time with him, other than the short drives to the restaurants and school, and she desperately wanted some.

When they pulled up in front of the Trestin's house, Eli got out and ran around and opened Maddie's door, but Jorge and Gabby stayed in the car. Maddie didn't know it, but the boys had made this plan earlier. Apparently, they wanted a little alone time with the girls, as well, even if it was only a couple of minutes.

Eli pulled Maddie to him as he leaned against the back of his car. "I really had a great time, Maddie."

"I did, too."

"And I had the prettiest date at the dance." Eli looked into Maddie's eyes.

"Well, I had the most handsome and most popular 'superstar' date." Maddie blushed.

"This has been the perfect weekend. First, the big win last night, and now the perfect evening with you."

"I never could have guessed I would end up here with you, Eli, when I started high school a few months ago. I don't know what you see in me. You know you could have any girl at school."

"First of all, that isn't true, Maddie. I couldn't have 'any girl' and don't want 'any girl'. I want you. You make me laugh, and more importantly, you understand me. I can talk to you about anything. I feel like there isn't anything I couldn't tell you."

"Same here," Maddie responded.

Then Eli leaned down and kissed her. And kissed her again. Maddie had never had a boy kiss her like this before. Then again, last year she was in middle school, and she didn't know any boys she wanted to kiss. When they stopped, she again lay her head on his chest. This was quickly becoming her favorite place to be. She felt a warmth and happiness spread through her. She didn't want to say goodbye, but she also had a curfew to make. Her parents had already extended it for the night, so she didn't want to break their trust.

She knocked on the back window. "Come on, Gabby. We better get inside."

"I don't want this night to end," she told Eli.

"But I guess it has to," he responded.

Eli and Jorge walked the girls to the front door and quickly gave them both quick pecks on the cheek. As they left, the girls quickly ran upstairs to Maddie's bedroom. They had so much to talk about!

30

Duncan's knee was slowly improving with his physical therapy, but his mood was not. He no longer needed his crutches to walk, but he did need something to boost his morale. Sheila called him into the family room where she was reading when he arrived home from school one afternoon.

"Duncan, let's talk." She patted the empty spot beside her on the sofa.

"What's up?"

"You tell me, Dunc. You seem to be miserable all the time. You rarely talk to us, and you haven't really even been seeing friends. You spend almost all of your time in your room, except when you are at school or at PT or you are eating."

"I'm fine, Mom."

"Duncan," Sheila pulled Duncan to her. "I know you were extremely disappointed about losing the end of your football season and your entire basketball season."

"And about hurting my knee."

"Of course, that, too. I know it's no fun being hurt or having to go to physical therapy, but I hate seeing you so sad."

"Mom—" Duncan struggled to hold back his tears. "I'm trying to be strong for you. How can I feel sorry for myself when you are going through what you are going through?"

"Oh, Duncan, honey. Of course, you can feel bad for yourself. You can even feel awful for yourself. You're allowed to be a little selfish when you go through an injury and lose what you lost."

"But you never complain about your cancer and your chemo. How can I complain or pout about my problems? That wouldn't be fair."

"It's not about being fair. None of this is fair. And it's wonderful that you are so concerned about my feelings. Maybe in the long run, what I am going through is worse than what you are going through right now. But this is a big deal for you; you lost something that you'd been counting down to. You are allowed to mourn for what you lost. That doesn't diminish what you're feeling for me and my situation."

Duncan finally let his tears go. He hadn't done that since the night he got home from the emergency room. He lay his head down on his mom's lap and cried for his own loss and for his mom. He'd been holding so much in that it felt good to let it all out.

"Thanks, Mom. I love you," he whispered up to her.

"I love you, too, buddy." Sheila thought for a minute. "Let's think of something to lift your spirits. You need something to do."

"But what? There isn't really anything I want to do but play basketball."

"And you can't do that. Hmmmm."

They both thought for a minute.

"I have an idea," Sheila perked up. "Why don't you go see the basketball coach before practice starts tomorrow? Maybe you can help out. Sort of like a team manager or something."

"They've already started the season, Mom."

"That's OK. It doesn't hurt to ask. He knows how excited you were to play and will understand why you want to be involved."

"I guess." Duncan didn't seem too excited.

"Plus, if you are at all the games and practices, look how much you will learn just by watching. I think you might be able to learn *more* by watching because you'll observe and listen and see the whole picture."

"Yeah?"

Sheila thought for a few seconds. She still needed a way to pull Duncan into her idea. "And think how impressed Coach will be with your dedication. That won't be lost on him next year. When he sees your talent next year and remembers your dedication from this year, you'll obviously be his favorite." She gave her son a wink.

"That's true!"

That had done it. "Thanks, Mom! I can be with all of my friends and be a part of the team!" he paused. "As long as Coach says it's OK."

"I can't imagine why he wouldn't. I guess you'll find out tomorrow."

Duncan stood up and grabbed his backpack to head to the other room.

"Now, why don't you go play some video games for a half hour or so? Give yourself a little fun. You need it."

"I do. But I'm starving, so I think I'll grab a sandwich first."

"Well, I guess you're feeling a little better already."

"What's for dinner?" he called out as he went into the kitchen.

31

Jake and Sheila were glad both Maddie and Duncan were in a good place emotionally when they decided it was time to talk to them about their move. Maddie was still flying high about Homecoming night and her relationship with Eli, and Duncan was also feeling much better, as the basketball coach had enthusiastically welcomed Duncan to the team in his amended role.

Lee was leaving the next day, so she decided to go all out and make a special dinner. She made short ribs, mashed potatoes, green beans with bacon, and homemade rolls. She even made a homemade apple pie for dessert. All comfort foods that the entire family would love.

Jake and Sheila had planned to talk to the kids during dinner, but when they saw the food on the table and everyone else's excitement at seeing it, they decided to enjoy the food first, and then talk later. Instead, they let Maddie and Duncan talk most of the dinner. They both had multiple good things to share that dinner. Maddie's good news focused on what she was doing with Eli that weekend if she were allowed, and she also shared her excitement about an A on her book report.

Duncan spent a lot of time talking about basketball practice. He thought the team was going to be good this year. "But they'd be a lot better with me," he explained.

"Next year," Jake assured him. "Maybe we can find a summer league for you so that you don't fall behind your teammates."

"Yeah! A summer league and maybe even camp."

"Great idea," Sheila agreed.

After dinner, Maddie and Duncan immediately started clearing the table and loading the dishwasher. They didn't need to be asked anymore; they both wanted to do whatever they could to help their parents. Luckily, Grammy Lee had washed pots, pans, and mixing bowls as she cooked, so that helped with the after-dinner cleanup.

"Thanks for a delicious dinner, Grammy," Maddie gave her a big hug.

"And for helping with the dishes!" Duncan quickly added.

"I sure am going to miss you all," Lee reached out and hugged Duncan as well.

"We'll all miss you, too," Jake added. "But you'll be back soon."

"And things will be very different then," Sheila decided it was time to transition into the difficult conversation.

"What do you mean?" Maddie inquired.

"Grammy won't be back until you are better?" Duncan questioned. "We thought she'd be back sooner than that."

"Well, let's hope your mother starts feeling better very soon, but that's not what she meant," Jake started the explanation. "You know I've been spending every spare moment looking for a new job, and I'm just not having very much luck."

"With all of my medical bills piling up, and all of our other many, many bills, we're going through a lot of money without replenishing it," Sheila tried to help Jake explain.

Jake jumped back in. "We've been thinking of ways to help save some money, and we've decided to rent out our house for a while. There's a place that manages short-term leases for people relocating to Chicago for business. They want to use our house. They can collect a lot of rent for a house like ours, and while they'll keep some of it as their commission, we'll get enough to make our house payment, pay rent on a temporary apartment, and even have a little left over for other bills."

Maddie and Duncan sat stunned, not knowing how to respond. They wanted to be supportive of their parents' decision, but they felt as though another rug was being yanked out from under them. Suddenly, the questions flew quickly:

"When do we have to go?"

"How long will we be gone?"

"What about all of our stuff?"

"What if they damage our house?"

"Who will make sure everything is OK here while we're gone?"

Jake listened as the kids threw out questions, then calmly tried to answer them all. "We'll take our personal belongings—our clothes, valuables, anything we definitely want with us and don't want anyone else to have access to."

"My Xbox and PlayStation?" Duncan questioned.

"Of course," Jake continued, "but all of our furniture, kitchen items, and other household essentials will stay here. We'll have all of that provided in our new apartment."

"Wait. Where are we moving?" Maddie wondered. "Did you already find a place?"

Sheila answered this question: "You know the apartment complex right by the school, Your Home Apartments?"

"Yeah, I know it. I always thought it was a pretty lame name. They couldn't think of anything better?"

Sheila laughed. "Well, that's now 'your home'."

"When are we going?" Duncan asked.

"And how big is the apartment?" Maddie inquired.

Jake looked at Duncan and answered his question first. "We are moving next weekend. Grammy has already been helping your mom pack some stuff, and Claire is going to come several days this week to help out, too."

Then he looked at Maddie. "The apartment has three bedrooms. We could have gotten a two-bedroom for a little less money, but we didn't think you two would get along too well sharing a room."

Jake and Sheila both laughed, while Duncan and Maddie both rolled their eyes at the thought.

Lee tried to help soften the blow a little, too. "A smaller place will be much easier to take care of while your mom isn't feeling so well. And you'll also be able to walk to school now. It's so close to the apartments that you won't have to worry about carpools and extra time to get to school. You can sleep a little later."

Both kids were in a bit of a daze when they went up to their rooms. Maddie ducked into Duncan's room for a minute to discuss the big news.

"How are you feeling about all of this, Duncan?" Maddie felt a little protective of her little brother in times of chaos.

"It's very weird. I've never lived anywhere else."

"I know, and I don't remember ever living anywhere else," Maddie paused, then added, "Duncan, I'm going to tell Gabby, of course, because I tell her everything, and she'd find out anyway, but let's not tell anyone else. They won't understand. It's a little embarrassing."

"OK. I guess we won't be having friends over anytime soon."

"Well, not after this week, anyway, and we don't really have friends over during the week."

"What are you going to tell Eli?" Duncan asked.

"I don't know, but DO NOT tell him if you see him, Duncan. I mean it."

"OK, OK. I won't. Calm down."

<h1 style="text-align:center">32</h1>

The move that weekend went off without a hitch. It really wasn't much more than packing for a long vacation, since most of their belongings were staying in the house "for strangers to use," Maddie had accidentally grumbled in front of her mom. Claire and Gabby had helped with much of the packing that week, and the management company was sending in a cleaning service once they were gone, so they didn't need to worry about that.

Once they had carried everything from their cars into their new "home", Maddie and Gabby shut themselves in Maddie's room, while Claire helped Sheila get settled.

"It's not so bad," Gabby reassured Maddie. "There's a basketball court for Duncan to practice on once he's well enough and a pool, so you won't be missing that next summer."

"Gabby! Please don't imply that we'll be here that long," Maddie scolded her.

"Well, you don't know what's going to happen. I know this sucks, but in the grand scheme of life, this isn't so bad." Gabby wasn't sure she believed everything she said, but she really wanted to be supportive of her best friend.

The girls were quiet as they took turns putting Maddie's clothes on hangers and hanging them in her closet. They then organized her shoes and dresser drawers with little more than small talk. Finally, Maddie broke the silence. "Please don't tell Jorge or anyone about this, Gabby."

"OK, it's your business to tell." Gabby hesitated. "How are you going to explain it to Eli?"

Maddie just kept working without answering that question.

"Maddie—" Gabby paused and looked at her friend straight in the face. "You have to tell Eli."

Maddie threw down the pile of socks she was putting into the top drawer, and they rolled all over the bedroom floor. "I don't, and I won't. I can't tell him. It's too embarrassing!"

Gabby walked over and grabbed Maddie by the shoulders. "Think about it. I'm not going to say anything to anyone, but you don't want Eli to find out some other way."

"How will he find out? I'm not telling him, you aren't telling, and Duncan isn't telling. I'm not telling *anyone* other than you, so no one will know."

"OK, but I still think it's a mistake. Eli doesn't care where you live. He likes you, Maddie, not your house and your yard and your pool."

"I know, I mean, I hope, but still—" Maddie's voice cracked, and she couldn't finish her thought. She knew she wasn't being fair to Eli and should trust him, but she just couldn't shake a feeling of shame, which made her feel even more ashamed for feeling that way. She felt so awful for her mom, who was suffering, and for her dad, who couldn't find a job, but the entire situation was just too much to handle.

She wanted to hold on to a little feeling of normalcy in her life.

"And you know there's nothing wrong with living in an apartment, Maddie."

"I know, that's not it." Maddie and Gabby had close friends who lived in apartments, and she didn't think less of them, but she couldn't shake the feeling she had. It had something to do with losing what she'd had her entire life.

"Well, I know you haven't forgotten that we have plans with Jorge and Eli tonight." The four of them had decided to see another movie in just a couple of hours.

"I already told Eli that I had family plans earlier in the day and that you and I would meet them there. I figured either your mom or my dad could take us, then the other could pick us up."

"OK, that's fine with me, but I'm on the record that this isn't a good idea. BUT—I'm here to support you and do what you think is best."

"Thanks, Gabby. You're the best." Maddie gave her best friend a huge hug.

33

Eli had only been home for about 30 minutes one afternoon when he picked up his phone to check social media and noticed he had an email. As a high school junior, he was continually getting emails from various colleges and universities. Usually, he didn't even bother opening them, but since this one was from the University of Michigan, a great school that was in his top three, he opened it immediately.

He couldn't believe his eyes when he saw it was from the football coach in charge of recruiting, who explained that they were interested in recruiting him to play for the Wolverines. The coach had actually been at one of the home games to see him play! He had no idea, and in hindsight, was glad he didn't know. He might have been too nervous. As he read on, he saw that the coach, along with the head coach, wanted to set up a time for him to visit campus.

Eli's first inclination was to text or call Maddie immediately after reading the email. Then he decided this news was too good not to share with her in person. Eli hadn't been to Maddie's house in several weeks, but he figured Maddie just hadn't asked him to come over because her mom was still undergoing chemo treatments and hadn't been feeling well. He knew Maddie was home, and it wasn't yet late in the evening, so he didn't think anyone would mind if he popped over and surprised Maddie.

He ran down the hall and hollered to his mom that he was running out for a couple of minutes, not even stopping to share the news with her. He planned to do that when he got home; he just couldn't wait to tell Maddie.

He pulled into the Trestin's driveway, ran to the front door, and rang the doorbell. A few seconds later, a woman he didn't recognize opened the door. Eli figured she was a family friend there to help out.

"Hi. Is Maddie home?" he anxiously asked.

"I'm sorry. No one named Maddie lives here," was the surprise answer.

"Yes, she does. Maddie Trestin. Who are you?"

"I can assure you Maddie Tresman does not live here. I do."

"It's Trestin, not Tresman. Do you know where the Trestins went? I didn't know they moved."

"I'm sorry. I don't know the Trestins. My family and I just relocated here from San Francisco, and we are renting this home."

"OK. I'm very confused but sorry to bother you. Have a good evening," Eli told the woman as he backed down the sidewalk.

"Thank you. You, too. Good luck finding her. I wish I could help."

Eli got into his car but didn't drive away immediately. He sat contemplating what had just happened and wondering why Maddie wouldn't have told him that she had moved. Before reaching out to Maddie, he texted Jorge to see whether Gabby had mentioned anything to him, but Jorge didn't know anything either.

Eli was a little shaken and didn't want to call Maddie, so he fired off a quick text: "Where r u?"

"At home."

"Where at home?"

"In my room. Y?"

"No. I mean what home? Im at ur house and some woman told me you don't live here!"

Maddie didn't answer right away because she didn't know what to say. She had been caught. Gabby had warned her not to hide her move from Eli, and now he had discovered it on his own.

"Y did u go to my house?"

"Avoiding the question Maddie."

Pause.

"Meet me at the diner in 30?"

"C u then."

Eli drove straight to the diner and had been there about 15 minutes when Maddie walked in.

"How did you get here? Who dropped you off?" Eli wondered.

"I walked here."

"Walked from where, Maddie? What's going on?"

Maddie sighed and looked down at her hands as they picked at her fingernails.

"My family moved, Eli."

"I know! Imagine my surprise when I showed up at your front door, or what *was* your front door, to surprise you with some good news, and some stranger told me you don't live there."

"I'm sorry, Eli. I know I should have told you."

"You think?" Eli was trying to be patient, but he was also angry. "All the hours we spend together and the hours we spend talking and texting when we aren't together, and you don't tell me when you move?"

"I was embarrassed. My dad lost his job, and we have a lot of medical bills piling up. He can't find a job, and he was worried about money, so we moved into an apartment."

"You sold the house? How did all of this happen so quickly?"

"We didn't sell the house," Maddie explained. "We are just renting it out because we can get a lot of money to help us with our bills." She still couldn't look Eli in the eyes.

"I still can't believe you didn't think you could tell me. Why?"

"I told you. I was embarrassed. I didn't know what you would think."

"Come on, Maddie. I thought you knew me better than that," Eli snapped. "From our very first phone conversation, I thought I made clear that I don't judge people by their color, their religion, *or* their economic circumstances. I mean—Mike is my best friend! He's being raised by his grandparents because his parents weren't up to it. They don't have a lot of money, and I don't care! I don't care about your money!"

Maddie sat in silence with tears running down her face.

"How do you think it makes me feel that you didn't trust me enough to tell me? And after I told you there wasn't anything I couldn't talk to you about," Eli continued.

"I'm sorry, Eli. Please don't be mad."

"I gotta go, Maddie. I don't know. I can't talk to you right now. I need to go."

"Wait! Eli! At least tell me what the good news is," her voice trailed off.

Eli didn't pause to answer her. Instead, he handed a $5 bill to the server to pay for his soda and left the diner. He didn't even look back inside to see what Maddie was doing. He drove away and left Maddie there to walk home.

34

Eli didn't call Maddie that night, nor did he talk to her at school the next day or the next or the next. Maddie felt as though she was living in a nightmare, with one bad thing happening after another. Maddie was certain she had fallen in love with Eli, and he had become her way of coping with all that was wrong in her life. She didn't know how to deal with the pain she was suffering, so she just floated through her day in a daze.

Gabby tried to console her, but nothing she said nor did could make Maddie feel better. Maddie knew she had done this to herself. Everything had been great with Eli, and she had deceived him. She was so worried about appearances that she hadn't been honest with him. It was both insulting and unfair to him, and he had done nothing but earn her trust.

"I wish I just knew why he went to the house to see me," she told Gabby one day at lunch.

"I know why. Are you sure you want to know?" Gabby questioned.

"Yes. Why?" Maddie's head jerked up, and she looked Gabby in the eyes.

"U Michigan wants him to play football."

"Are you kidding?" Maddie's spirits lifted for a quick moment, as she was excited for Eli. Then her mood quickly crashed again as she realized he hadn't even shared the good news with her yet. He had such great news, but he was still too mad at her to tell her. She had really blown it and realized she might not get Eli back.

Maddie knew this was a dream come true for him and wanted to congratulate Eli, but she couldn't force herself to walk up to him. He wouldn't even look at her when she saw him in the hallway. Finally, she decided to send him a quick text. What more harm could that do?

"Congrats," she sent.

Three dots, then nothing, then three dots, then nothing. Finally, he answered with a quick "thanks".

"Im really excited for u!" she texted.

"Not ready yet Maddie," was all he sent back.

Maddie knew she had better stop texting and ran to the bathroom crying. She stood in the stall sobbing silently for several minutes before pulling off a long strand of toilet paper to blow her nose and wipe her face. She had one more class to get through before she could go home, but instead of listening and writing notes as she should have done in class, she sat daydreaming about Eli being a star athlete at Michigan, trying to convince herself that she still would be a part of it.

When Maddie got home that afternoon, she found her mom curled up on her bed. Sheila wasn't feeling well and had spent part of the afternoon on the bathroom floor.

"Where's Dad?" Maddie asked.

"He ran to the store. Will you lie down beside me for a little bit? I need a snuggle."

"Of course," Maddie answered and curled up with her mom. She hadn't told Sheila about the apparent breakup with Eli because she didn't want her to worry about her. Suddenly, Maddie felt like a little girl wrapped in her mother's arms again, and somehow, she felt a little better.

"Will you sing to me?" Sheila asked her.

Maddie had taken piano and voice lessons when she was younger, and Sheila used to love when she would sing. She had such a beautiful voice, and Sheila wished Maddie hadn't given up on her musical talents.

Maddie knew exactly what song she wanted to sing. She sang the entire Air Supply song to Sheila. She had studied and quickly learned *All Out of Love* after Eli shared his story about the song and its importance to him.

"That was beautiful, sweetheart," Sheila praised her daughter when the song ended. Then she managed a little laugh. "Maybe an interesting choice of song, but it was beautiful."

Maddie gave her mom a little smile. She couldn't believe she had made it through the song without crying, but she couldn't really think of anything else but her mom at that minute.

They cuddled on the bed for a little longer, and before either of them knew it, they were both asleep. Neither moved for about 30 minutes and then Maddie suddenly jerked awake. She was getting uncomfortable, and her neck was starting to hurt, but she was afraid to move because she didn't want to disturb her mom. Finally, she very slowly moved Sheila's arms and crawled out from her hug.

She was sneaking out of the room when Sheila called to her, "Maddie, will you please start singing again? Isn't there a choir or something at school you can join?"

"Actually, there are a few of them, Mom." Maybe that's what she needed—something to take her mind off Eli. "And I think that's a good idea. Would that make you happy?"

"Yes, it would."

"Then I'll do it. I think it would make me happier, too." Maddie wasn't ready to give up on Eli, but she realized she needed something to preoccupy her and pull her out of her funk. She also couldn't help but hope that Eli would notice she had found something new in her life.

"Happier? Aren't you happy, Maddie? I know this move has been disappointing for you."

Maddie walked back over and sat down on the side of the bed. It was time to come clean and share her mistakes with her mom.

"I haven't been very happy, Mom. I'm not happy about your cancer; I'm not happy about Dad losing his job; I'm not happy about leaving our home." She paused to gather strength. "And I'm not happy that I screwed everything up with Eli." She wanted to share what she was going through, but she couldn't look her mom in her eyes while she explained it.

"I'm so sorry you've been going through this, honey. I wish you had told me."

"I know, Mom, but I didn't want to burden you with my pain—and my stupidity. I know I shouldn't be embarrassed about living here, and I definitely shouldn't have been so stupid to try to hide it from Eli."

"It's hard being a teenager, Maddie. And as fun and wonderful as it can be, it's also hard being in high school, wondering who's judging you and who's wishing for you to fail, especially when you are dating a handsome and successful star athlete."

Maddie sat silently listening, so Sheila continued, "You are going to make many mistakes, not only in high school but also all through life. You can be sad about mistakes, but you need to learn not to dwell on them but instead to learn from them. Mistakes are an important part of growing up, and of growing as a person. If we don't recognize our mistakes and learn from them, how can we become better people?"

"Wise words, Mom, but easier said than done," Maddie told Sheila as she gave her a hug.

"I know. So true. How about you give Eli a little space? Once he calms down, he'll probably want to talk this out with you. He cares about you, but you really hurt his feelings. Give it some time to see whether he comes to you."

"OK. In the meantime," Maddie sang to a little tune, "I think I'll look into a choir or other music group at school. It could help take my mind off everything."

"I think that's a superb idea. And I'll be happy to hear your beautiful voice again."

"Thanks, Mom. I better get some homework done. I'm afraid my mind hasn't been in it lately."

35

Maddie finished her schoolwork, then decided to do her research into the various choirs, bands, and acapella groups at school. She logged onto the Clubs and Activities page on the school website and found that several of the groups were already full for the semester but that she could join a newly formed stage band that included vocalists.

She didn't know any of the other kids but thought it might be a nice opportunity to meet and make some other friends at school. By hanging out with a totally new group of kids, she wouldn't constantly be reminded of Eli. Of course, she wouldn't abandon Gabby and her other friends, but it would be nice to have some new ones as well.

Maddie walked into her first practice with the group, a little nervous (actually very nervous, as she would tell Sheila later) but with confidence. She knew she had a pleasant singing voice, though a little unpracticed. She had started some singing exercises to strengthen her vocal cords and improve her range.

The group practiced several popular songs from across decades, everything from the Beatles to the Rolling Stones to Cold Play to Imagine Dragons. Maddie loved it! She got lost in the music and really enjoyed herself as the kids laughed and joked as they worked on the songs.

At the end of practice, Jason, a senior and the group leader, announced a surprise. There would be a large all-school assembly on the last day of school before spring break, and they had been asked to perform.

"Two things before we leave for the day," Jason announced. "First, it's time we come up with a name, so everyone brainstorm and come with some ideas for the next time we meet. Second, I think we sound great performing the covers we've been working on, but wouldn't it be fun if we could come up with an original song?"

"That's very ambitious," someone yelled out.

"It is ambitious, and I'm not saying it's a must, but if any of us wants to work on it, it could be fun," Jason assured. "I'm game. Anyone else?"

Jason played guitar, both electric and acoustic. Annie, the keyboardist/pianist, chimed in that she'd be willing to try.

"I know I'm new here, but I'll give it a shot," Maddie bravely volunteered.

"So will I," a shy sophomore named Max spoke in a loud whisper.

"Great," Jason was pleased to see his volunteers. "We'll set up some time to meet outside of our regular practices, but in the meantime, why don't we all tinker around with some lyrics and melodies? See everyone next time."

Maddie couldn't wait to get home and start brainstorming some ideas. She had never written a song before, but she certainly had many emotions to pull from right now. Love, loss, sickness, health, mistakes, strength—

she had a myriad of subjects from which to choose. She decided she'd just see what came to mind. The lyrics flowed out very quickly and without much thought:

I'm sitting here without you,
And thinking about what I've done.
I can't say I'm proud of myself,
Or the person I've become.

I've made too many mistakes,
And I know I'm far from done.
But I promise to grow and learn,
And hope I can be the one.

The one who's by your side
The one who holds your hand
The one who lifts you up
The one who gives you strength
With you, our one plus one
Can equal, not two, but one.

I hope that you'll forgive me,
And help me learn to grow.
We can overcome together,
To you I certainly owe.

So let's start over again,
Let Cupid shoot his bow.
Our love can start anew,
And be better than before. Oh!

The one who's by your side
The one who holds your hand
The one who lifts you up
The one who gives you strength
With you, our one plus one
Can equal, not two, but one.

Maddie read through the song and settled on the title *One Plus One Equals One*, then thought that might be too long, so she shortened it to *One Plus One*. Then she second-guessed herself again and thought she'd wait to see what the others thought. "I wonder whether they'll even like it," she said to herself.

She was pleased with her first attempt at songwriting but realized she would need help with the music portion of it. She couldn't wait to sit down with Jason, Annie, and Max to see what they could all do with it together.

She quickly looked up their email addresses in the school directory and sent them the lyrics. She also included her phone number so that they could start a text chain.

Jason was the first to text. "That was quick! Nice goin."

Annie added, "Sounds like someone is going thru something."

Maddie agreed, "Guess I gave it away."

Then Max jumped in. "I really like it."

Jason asked, "Can everyone meet on Thursday after school?"

So it was set. They were going to work on the song together. Maybe they'd need to tweak some things, but Maddie had actually written a song! She felt better than she'd felt in what felt like a long time.

36

Maddie's session with Jason, Annie, and Max was going great. Jason and Annie were so talented on their instruments, and even Max was opening up and sharing some great ideas. The four of them had decided on their own that they should be the ones to be featured in this song in the concert since they were the ones putting in the work and writing the song.

It was only fair. Jason would play acoustic guitar, and Annie would play piano, while Maddie and Max would do the vocals. Maddie and Max had voices that complemented each other very well, so Maddie would sing the verses alone, while Max would join in and harmonize for the refrain. They would feature a piano solo after the first chorus, then a guitar solo after the second chorus, then they would repeat the chorus a third time.

Maddie had decided not to tell her parents, Duncan, or even Gabby about the song. She had totally gotten lost in the process, and it had been a great distraction from life's pains. She wanted to surprise all of them by inviting them to the concert, which was quickly approaching.

While Maddie was practicing and working with Jason, Annie, and Max one afternoon after school, Duncan was in the gym carefully shooting hoops with some boys from the basketball team.

The season was over, and Duncan had had a great experience working with the team, but he was ready for a more active role. He couldn't play basketball quite yet, and he knew he had to be careful, but his knee was recovering well, and he was able to shoot from different spots around the arch. He wanted to practice his shots and stay as fresh as possible so that he'd be ready for his summer league in just a few months.

Unbeknownst to Maddie and Duncan, while they were enjoying their after-school activities, Jake and Sheila were in the oncologist's office. What seemed like never-ending rounds of chemotherapy and radiation had finally come to an end for Sheila. They sat holding hands and waiting for the results of her most recent tests.

Dr. Beckham walked in with a smile. "How about some good news, Sheila?"

"I'm certainly not going to say no to that!"

"And no need for suspense," Jake added.

"You are cancer-free!" Dr. Beckham exclaimed.

Sheila and Jake looked at each other. "Thank God," they both whispered, then quickly hugged each other in relief.

"What are the chances this is going to come back?" Jake was the first to ask. He didn't want his wife, nor the rest of the family, going through this again. "Can this just be behind us as a bad memory, please?"

"I would love to tell you that is *definitely* the case, but I can't do that. As you know, we caught your cancer very early, Sheila, and that greatly increases your chances. People are people, not statistics, and it all gets very confusing, but on average, people who are treated in Stage 1 have a 5-year survival rate of 90%. The longer you go cancer-free, the greater your chances are. Once we get 15 to 30 years past your treatment, without relapse, there's a very good chance something else will get you before the cancer does."[1]

"You're right. That is confusing. So—chances are good?" Shelia asked for clarification.

"Yes, very good," Dr. Beckham reassured her, then proceeded to break down more statistics and explain how they would monitor her over the next months and years to make sure Sheila remained healthy.

As Jake and Sheila drove home, they decided they needed to celebrate. They were both "starving" because neither of them had had an appetite before the consultation with Dr. Beckham, but rather than stopping for food, they rushed home to the apartment. They wanted to be there when their kids got home. They had just gotten there and were freshening up when Maddie and Duncan walked in.

"We're home," Maddie called out as she opened the door.

"And I'm starving!" Duncan called out.

"So are we," Sheila answered as she and Jake walked out of the bedroom.

"But before we eat, sit down for a minute. Your mom and I want to tell you something." Jake gestured to the sofa.

"Oh no. What now?" Maddie questioned.

---

[1] Eldridge, Lynne, MD, "Rising Survival Rates with Hodgkin Lymphoma: Understanding Your Prognosis with Hodgkin Disease," verywellhealth.com, Updated May 22, 2020.

"Not more bad news, please," Duncan pleaded.

"Not bad news at all," Sheila assured them with a grin.

"Your mom and I just got back from the doctor, and she's cancer-free!" Jake's voice cracked.

"Yippee!" Maddie yelled, as she and Duncan both jumped up and ran to their parents. They all took turns hugging each other before concluding with one big four-way group hug.

"Does that mean you are totally cured, Mom?" Duncan asked with hope.

"Well, at least for now—" Sheila started.

"What?" both kids questioned simultaneously.

"Nothing is ever for sure, but my chances are very, very good," Sheila finished her thought.

"Your mom plans on living a very long life," Jake said, then quickly changed the subject. "We decided we all deserve a nice celebratory dinner out tonight, so where do you want to go?"

"Wherever it is, can we go soon?" Duncan pleaded.

"We can go right now," Sheila told him.

"How about McGuire's for a good ribeye?" Maddie asked with raised eyebrows. She felt a little guilty about choosing an expensive steak house.

"I think I could use the protein," Sheila laughed. "Why don't you both go change into something a little nicer, and I'll call to see whether we can get in?"

37

The auditorium was packed, and Maddie didn't think she had ever been this nervous as she peeked out from behind the curtains to see whether her parents were there yet. She searched the standing-room-only edges of the room because she knew the seats would be filled with students. Sure enough, she found Jake and Sheila standing in the back.

She couldn't resist the urge, and her eyes quickly scanned the area where Eli would be sitting with his friends. It was easy to find him because each class had its own designated section in the auditorium, and Eli and Mike always sat in the exact same seats. Much to her chagrin, they were surrounded by a group of senior girls giggling and flirting.

"Stop looking," Maddie scolded herself. "Focus." She quickly shut the curtains and went farther backstage to do some breathing exercises and warm-up chords.

Max walked up behind her. "Are you ready, Maddie?"

"Geez, Max. You scared me. I didn't hear you coming."

"Sorry."

"That's OK. I'm ready. How about you?"

"I'm very nervous. I can't believe I agreed to this," Max confessed.

"Max, you have a great voice. It's normal to be nervous, but you really have nothing to worry about. And I can't do it without you!"

"Thanks, Maddie."

"Plus, we have our cover songs first, so we'll be warmed up and will have gotten our nerves flushed out by the time we get to our song."

"Yeah, I guess," Max agreed.

"Let's practice our duet really quick," Maddie urged him.

By the time they had sung through their refrain twice, it was time to line up on stage. Maddie grabbed Max's hand and gave it a quick squeeze. She wasn't sure whether she was trying to calm his nerves or her own.

As they sang through their first four songs, Maddie looked mostly at her parents while she sang. She wasn't sure why, but looking at them calmed her nerves. She had no urge to look toward Eli. She did wonder, though, whether he was surprised to see her up there. She didn't know whether he realized she had joined the group.

Their fourth cover song came to an end, and Jason lifted his microphone to speak:

"Thank you all for being here today, not that you really had a choice, I guess. For those of you who don't know, our group, The Titan Tunes, is new this year. We've had a lot of fun preparing these songs for you, but to end things, we'd like to share an original song. Our newest member, Maddie Trestin, wrote the lyrics, while Annie Lee and I wrote the music, along with the help of Maddie and Max Trumble. It's called *One Plus One Equals One,* and the four of us will perform it now. We hope you enjoy it. Thanks, and have a great spring break!"

Maddie hardly had time to be shocked that Jason had given her the writing credit in front of the entire school when Annie started the music. Jason soon joined in, and then it was her turn.

"I'm sitting here without you, And thinking about what I've done," she began, and before she could even believe it, the song was over and the crowd erupted into cheers and applause. She looked out and saw Eli and Mike stand up, then she looked over at Gabby and saw her stand up. Soon, the entire audience was standing and applauding. Maddie and Max looked at each other with grins from ear to ear. The four of them took a quick bow, then Jason motioned for the rest of the group to stand and bow. And with that, everyone started a quick exit from the auditorium.

Instead of leaving, Gabby ran up to Maddie and gave her a huge hug. "Oh my God, Maddie, that was incredible. You didn't tell me you wrote a song! How could you not tell me that?"

"I wanted to surprise you, but I didn't actually know Jason was going to tell everyone."

"Did you see Eli, Maddie? He was the first person to stand up and cheer after the song was over."

"Yeah, that was nice." Maddie looked down at the floor.

Then Jake and Sheila made their way to the stage as well.

"Maddie, we are so proud of you. That was amazing!" Jake beamed with pride at his daughter.

Sheila hugged her. "That was a beautiful song, Maddie. We had no idea."

"She didn't tell you either?" Gabby asked, surprised.

"Thanks, everyone." Maddie couldn't help but look around. She was very excited about the performance and how her song seemed to be a hit, but she also couldn't help but feel a little melancholy that it was over, and even more so, that Eli hadn't come to congratulate her afterward.

"We actually better get going if we want to eat lunch before we have to get to class," Maddie tugged on Gabby. "Thanks for coming, Mom and Dad. It really helped my nerves seeing you in the crowd."

"Glad we could be of service," Jake teased her.

"Bye, honey. Congratulations again. We are so proud of you. Oh! Are you coming home after school, or do you have plans?" Sheila inquired.

"I'll let you know," Maddie hollered as she and Gabby left for the cafeteria. "Gabby and I might just get a coffee or something after school."

"OK. Have a good rest of the day."

38

Instead of coffee, Maddie and Gabby decided to get ice cream after school. It was now officially spring break, after all, so they decided to celebrate their next 2 weeks of freedom.

"Also," Gabby urged her best friend, "you need ice cream to celebrate your big performance today. And I need ice cream to celebrate that I'm best friends with a pop star."

"Haha, Gabby. You're a goof." Maddie rolled her eyes.

They ordered their cones—Maddie got chocolate chip cookie dough, while Gabby ordered mint chip—and they sat on the bench in front of the shop eating them. They started making a verbal list of everything they wanted to do over break.

"There are a few things Jorge and I decided we want to do. I wish you and Eli were still together so that you could go with us," Gabby pouted.

"It's OK. You guys go have fun. What were you thinking of doing?"

"A bunch of things, Six Flags, mini golf, ice skating. Of course, some of that depends on the weather. It is the end of March, you know, but I think we're supposed to have some decent weather."

Gabby texted Claire and asked her to come get her. When she arrived, Claire told Maddie to jump in the car. It was only a couple of blocks to the apartment, but Claire said there was no need for Maddie to walk when it would only take 30 seconds to drop her off.

Gabby climbed out of the car with Maddie and gave her a quick squeeze. "I'm sorry I have plans with Jorge tonight, or I would hang out with you. We planned this movie a couple of weeks ago."

"It's fine, Gabby. I'm glad you're going. I'm actually exhausted from everything today, anyway. I'll talk to you tomorrow. Have fun."

"OK, bye."

"Bye, Maddie," Claire yelled from inside the car.

Maddie walked in the door to the apartment and quickly dropped her backpack. She couldn't believe her eyes. She saw her parents quickly retreat to their bedroom, but sitting on the sofa in front of her was Eli. She didn't know what to say and just stared at him.

Eli looked back at Maddie with a soft grin. "I guess we have a new song," he almost whispered as he stood and walked to Maddie.

"Who—What—How did you know where we live?" Maddie finally spit out.

"I shot Duncan a text and asked him. Then I made him promise he wouldn't tell you," Eli explained.

"That has to be the first time Duncan has ever kept a secret in his entire life."

"Well, I guess he didn't have to keep it very long. I asked him after school, then I came right here. I should have known you would do something after school, but it was nice catching up with your parents. Your mom looks fantastic. I'm so glad she's doing well."

"Yeah. It's a big relief for all of us. Her cancer is in remission, and there's a very good chance she beat it for good."

"Thank God," Eli sighed.

"Sooooo—" Maddie looked at Eli in search of answers.

"Maddie, that was a beautiful song. I didn't know— your voice is incredible. And I loved the song."

"Well, I had a good inspiration for it."

"I have a feeling that was written with me in mind?" Eli said, as a question rather than a statement.

"You think?" Maddie laughed. "What would ever give you that idea?"

Eli laughed. "But I don't want you to think that's the only reason I'm here. I've planned all week to talk to you. I have some news I want to share, and I haven't told a soul yet. I didn't get to share my news the last time, so you get to be first this time."

"Are you sure you don't want to tell those girls I saw flirting with you in the auditorium today?" Maddie smiled but blushed as she asked, feeling embarrassed that she even brought it up.

"The keywords there, Maddie, are 'flirting with you'— or with me. They were flirting. I was merely listening and talking. And Mike was flirting!"

They both laughed.

"I know I shut you out, Maddie, but you have no idea how hurt I was."

"I'm really sorry, Eli."

"I know you are, but I'm really sorry, too. I should have been a little more understanding. You were going through a lot with your mom being sick, and having to leave your home, and having so much uncertainty and pain. I don't know how I would have handled it, either."

"Then what took you so long?" Maddie half-joked with Eli.

"Well, it took me a while to make these realizations because I was focused on my own anger and pain, and to be honest, I was embarrassed at how I had acted, and I wasn't sure how you would respond if I came crawling back to you."

"I'm glad you finally decided to take the chance." Maddie reached out and grabbed both of his hands as she got closer to him. "Now, how about that good news?"

A huge grin spread across Eli's face. "I committed to Michigan. I'm going to be a Wolverine!"

"That's fantastic, Eli!" Before she knew what she was doing, Maddie jumped up, wrapped her arms around Eli's neck and shoulders, and kissed him. And he kissed her back. It all seemed so natural, as though nothing had ever happened between them.

"I mean, I still have to apply and send in my SATs, but it's pretty much a sure thing."

"And Michigan isn't even that far. It's in Ann Arbor, right?"

"Yep."

Maddie laughed. "Since we are being totally honest with each other from now on, I have to admit that I already checked directions and distance from here to Ann Arbor."

"Oh, you did, huh?" Eli leaned down and kissed Maddie again. Then he added, "But we still have the rest of this year and my entire senior year before we have to worry about that."

"Yes. So much to look forward to." Maddie wasn't sure she had ever felt happier.

"Oh! Speaking of things to look forward to, how about going to the movie with Jorge and Gabby tonight?" Eli asked.

"I can't wait to tell Gabby we are back together!"

"Sorry, Maddie. I'm guessing she already knows. Or at least has an idea. Jorge knew I was coming over here, but I guess they had no way of knowing whether you'd just kick me out or take me back with open arms."

"No, I'm pretty sure Gabby knows I wouldn't do that. She knows my arms would be wide open."

"Shall we let your family come out of their hiding places?" Eli laughed.

"Not yet! One more kiss!"

Acknowledgements

Thank you to my husband, Francois; our son, Lachlan; and our daughter, Sloan, undoubtedly three of the smartest and most-talented people I know. Their success gave me the confidence to finally write this book.

Thank you to my great niece, Madalynn, and my niece, Daphne, for use of the name Maddie. While Madalynn does not use the nickname, Maddie, we all know what Maddie's real name is. I chose the name more than a decade before Madalynn was born—a sign of great things to come.

Thanks to my 8th grade English teacher, gymnastics coach, and friend, Cynthia Snow. From the time she chose me for the Young Author's conference, she knew I would write a book; she just didn't think it would take me 40 years.

Thanks to the Mayo Clinic's website (mayoclinic.org) for providing me with some general information about Hodgkin's lymphoma and to Lynne Eldridge, MD, and her article "Rising Survival Rates with Hodgkin Lymphoma: Understanding Your Prognosis with Hodgkin Disease", verywellhealth.com, Updated May 22, 2020, for additional information.

Thanks to the soft rock duo *Air Supply* for use of their song. *All Out of Love* was one of my favorites in middle school.

Thanks to Sloan and my friend, Merrill Simpson, for helping me through the arduous process of choosing a book title.

Thanks also to the rest of my family: my parents, Terry and Vanda Lawrence; Lisa; Mark; Elena; my in-laws, Francois and Gladys Charles; Dominique; Danielle; David; and Tim—just for being you.